WHEN A LIONESS HUNTS

A LION'S PRIDE #8

EVE LANGLAIS

CHAPTER ONE

The cat, a definite look of malice in its eyes, swiped at him, and Theodore only barely managed to dodge the sharp claws. The evil beast yowled and hissed, expressing its disappointment at the lack of blood.

Theodore kind of wanted to growl right back but instead wound up sneezing. Again. Damned allergies.

This was why he didn't have pets.

Achoo. The third time, strategically aimed, proved a charm, given the fluffy white devil bolted, scattering even more of the papers on the table. Utility bills. Some of them with stains. Crumpled receipts. Coupons joined the mix as well, along with a few recipes, colorful pages ripped from magazines.

A mess. It was almost enough to make him twitch. He certainly required a lint brush. The hair sticking to him appeared stark on the dark fabric of his pants. A good thing he kept a spare pair in his trunk. He'd have to change before he got into his car.

Mrs. Peterson—a lady in her eighties, according to her date of birth—tottered from the kitchen with a cup of tea shaking and sloshing in one hand, a plate of cookies in the other. She set the beverage in front of him. The hot liquid had a hair floating on the top.

There'd been a time early in his career that he would have gagged. Now he calmly said, "Thank you," and proceeded to ignore it.

She set the plate of cookies—probably made in a hair-and-dander-dusted kitchen—alongside.

His stomach shriveled into a terrified ball. No way was he eating or drinking. He didn't care how widely the old lady beamed or how excited she was as she exclaimed, "They're homemade."

Given cat hair appeared to blanket her home, that wasn't exactly a ringing endorsement.

"This is very nice, Mrs. Peterson, but you were supposed to fetch your receipts. Remember, the ones detailing these deductions?" He pointed to the small script on the form. The writing was shaky in many places except where there were large refunds to be had. Those numbers were quite clear and sizeable, belonging to receipts he'd yet to see.

Mrs. Peterson kept stalling under the guise of hospitality. He didn't buy it for one minute.

"I can assure you, all of those deductions were necessary medical procedures," she said, sitting in the chair across from him and watching his cup of tea intently.

"Which means you have details, billing records. As mentioned before, I need to see them."

"Do you think I'm lying? I would never," she huffily declared. She quickly changed the subject. "You haven't drunk your tea."

"I'm not thirsty, nor am I accusing you of anything, Mrs. Peterson, but I will require more than your word that these medical expenses exist."

She lifted her nose. "I swear, today's youth is all rush, rush, rush. No sense of manners at all. In my day, we had a nice cup of tea before getting down to business."

He sighed. "Mrs. Peterson, as I've already told you, this isn't a social call."

"And isn't that the problem these days? No one has time to talk anymore. Everyone glued to their phones and that internet thing." She sniffed.

"Mrs. Pet—"

Ding. Dong.

"What do you know. Visitors. It better not be my ungrateful son and that whore."

The whore being her daughter-in-law of thirty-five years. He'd already heard all about them. He understood why they didn't visit.

Saved by the bell. Mrs. Peterson tottered to the front door to answer it. Theodore took a moment to grab that damnable cup of disgusting dirty water and dump it in the nearest thing he spotted. The cat's water bowl changed color as he poured. He was upright and pretending to hold the empty cup to his lips when Mrs. Peterson returned.

"Sorry for the interruption. Someone wanted to check my water meter despite that nice fellow who came just last month."

"You shouldn't let them in your house." He set the cup down, and she eyed it with a sly smile.

"Now there's a good boy."

"If we could get to business. The receipts. Now." He added some firmness to his request.

"I am sorry, but just like I told the last fellow from the IRS, I don't have them. Because they don't exist." Stated quite boldly and without a hint of a quiver in her voice. "The government are bloody vultures thinking they can claw at the pension my husband gave me."

"I am not here to debate our laws."

"But you are here to enforce them."

"You didn't give us a choice. You got a refund of seventy-five thousand dollars." Which raised the first set of flags at the office.

"And? I just filled out the papers like I was supposed to," she defended.

"You only had an income of thirty thousand."

"Because that company my dear Gordie worked for screwed its employees." She scowled.

A flash of movement showed the feline lapping at its water bowl. It liked the tea, probably because it was flavored with cat hair.

"I am not here about the amount of your pension but the fact you demanded a return for a paid receipt that exceeded it, which is quite impossible given you claim to have no assets other than this house."

She sighed and rolled her eyes dramatically. "And this is why the last fellow is now composting in the basement."

"Did you just admit to the murder of my missing colleague?" he asked softly, not relaying any hint of his emotions.

"Yes, I did." Stated quite proudly. "And you're about to join him. It's your own fault really. Bothering an old lady in her golden years." She sniffed. "You should use the sparse time you have left to reflect on your poor decision to work for the government."

"And how will you eliminate me?" he asked.

"I already have with that tea you drank!" Her expression turned sly. "I poisoned it. You'll be dead in a few minutes."

"Is this where I should admit I didn't drink the tea? Your cat did." He gestured and wished he'd worn a camera. Because the situation erupted.

Mrs. Peterson screeched, "Baby! No."

The old lady dove from her chair and scooped up the cat grooming himself nearby. The thing yowled and tore out of her arms.

"I don't think he drank much. We can call a vet once we've concluded our business."

"We won't be concluding shit you—you—cat

hater!" Mrs. Peterson grabbed a knitting needle from her basket and jabbed at him.

He batted the wand aside and, after a scuffle that indicated he needed to spend more time in the gym, subdued the tax fraudster. He felt no guilt at all as he handcuffed her. She could glare all she wanted. She'd broken the law.

"You should have been the one to drink it," she spat.

"You should have stuck to legitimate deductions," he said.

Mrs. Peterson, who'd been perpetrating income tax fraud for a while now, went to jail. The cat, despite his thoughts on the matter, was saved.

A job well done, Theodore went home—in a spare outfit, his filthy suit bagged. It immediately went into the dry cleaning pile once he got home, and he took a long shower with plenty of soap to ensure not a trace of feline remained on him.

He hated cats. His grandmother used to have a houseful when he was growing up. The nasty things didn't like the little boy that came to live with their owner. Peeing on his pillow. Scratching all his things. When he developed allergies, his grandmother had him shipped to boarding school. Which turned out to be a good thing.

Theodore enjoyed the structure and neatness of the academy. He credited them for the man he became. A man who thrived on order. Not chaos. Rules gave Theodore the boundaries he needed.

The day after he took down Mrs. Peterson, he was called to Garry Maverick's office. One of the higher-ups in the bureau who had been giving Theodore more interesting assignments, lately. He hoped that meant he'd soon get the promotion he'd been working hard for.

"Theo, good job on the pregnant granny case." Because not only had Mrs. Peterson claimed a massive refund she wasn't entitled to, she'd chosen to claim it was because she'd had twins. She might have been shown leniency if she'd not tried to eliminate the agent sent to question her.

"Did you find the other agent, sir?"

"We did." Maverick, the man who'd handpicked Theodore for the job, looked somber. "Barely alive because of the poison but recovering now in the hospital. Good job."

"Thank you, sir." As if he'd ever call this steely-eyed man anything else.

"So, Loomer"—the use of last names common in the office—"you've been showing promise on the more complicated cases I've been assigning you. What if I said we have something big we'd like you to take a look at? Give us your thoughts."

"Another field case?" Theodore straightened in his seat. He'd only recently been given the chance to go on field assignments. Until now, he'd been an internal auditor, which he didn't mind. Numbers had an orderly fashion to them that he quite enjoyed. He'd cracked many a case without ever leaving the office.

However, he could admit to a certain excitement of escaping the sterile office to work for Maverick himself, a man spoken of in hushed tones.

"We think it might be a huge one." Maverick slid the file over.

Theodore popped it open and noticed it contained several files. A quick scan showed a few things immediately. "According to the address in these filings, they all live in the same place."

"It's a massive condominium downtown. Very restricted in who gets to live there."

Theodore tapped his finger on the file. "I see a few share the same last name. I assume they're family."

"Pretty much everyone in that condo is related in some way. Given the number of incidences, we think the whole family is involved in the scam, and it extends well beyond the taxes."

But using the taxes as an excuse would get them in for a closer look and probably give them cause for warrants and such.

"Did you see anything that sticks out?" Theodore asked.

"Not really other than they're private. Preliminary digging hasn't found much. They have very little social media presence. Odd in this day and age."

"Maybe they like to be unplugged." Theodore certainly wasn't one to indulge in electronic entertainment. Computers were for work. When he relaxed, he preferred to read a classic or cook.

"They also believe in creative accounting. They've been dodging taxes for years now."

"Nothing big, though," Theodore remarked as he thumbed through the folder. "All the refunds are under ten grand."

"But take a look at what they're classing as business deductions."

Theodore frowned. "That's an awful lot of expense for something that's not making money."

"It gets better," Maverick said. "When receipts were requested, they sent some in."

Flipping to the back of the folder, he saw scanned copies of crumpled receipts. Some of them blatantly inadmissible. How could anyone claim a manicure and pedicure were needed for work?

"What's with the biggest expenses? It doesn't actually say what company sold these things or what it actually is." He pointed to a typed receipt with a stream of digits and letters, almost like a model number. In another column, a quantity of ten thousand, then a hefty dollar amount.

"We aren't sure what that's supposed to be, but we'd like to find out. It might be related to the bigger things I mentioned."

Theodore kept skimming. "All these files are for females ranging in age from early twenties to the fifties."

"A pair in there seem to be mother and daughter. Another two, possibly cousins."

"Marital status is mixed. As are living conditions," Theodore noted.

"Roommates and spouses mean there could be more people involved."

Theodore snapped the folder shut. "I'll do some research, start some inquiries, and then make some appointments with the subjects."

"Already done. The letters informing them they're being audited have already been sent with appointment times recorded. None called to reschedule. The first is tomorrow afternoon. Melly Goldeneyes."

"This is short notice," Theodore remarked, remembering with his eidetic memory the file Maverick referred to. The one with the name Melly had a driver's license picture attached and not a very flattering one. She squinted and had her hair going every which way, as if she'd just emerged from a tornado.

"I'm sure you'll manage. We need this handled."

"I'll handle it, but why the urgency? Won't that be suspicious?" The IRS wasn't known to be a fast-moving machine.

"Because we have reason to believe animals might be in danger."

Given he wasn't crazy about beasts of any kind, his first impulse was not the kind he'd admit out loud. "If you believe that, then why not conduct a raid?"

"Because the situation is delicate. We can't just rush in without concrete proof. The repercussions..." Maverick shook his head. "We have to be sure. Resolve this quickly and you can have a few days off."

Days off to do what? He had nothing left to clean, and even he could get tired of reading.

"You can count on me."

Theodore spent that day and the next reading the files, making notes, planning exactly what to ask. He made a list of questions. Numbered them and added sub lists to a few. He'd show Maverick he could keep doing fieldwork.

The day of the appointment, he circled the building a few times, watching it as he crept past. It projected into the sky, a big golden high-rise with a wall all around it.

Given the road bypassing the condo had no parking, he had to resort to a garage a few blocks over. The spot between a pillar and a wall with no one at his back provided the utmost protection for his car.

As he walked to the address on file, he chose the sidewalk side that ran the length of the massive wall. It extended the length of the block and turned the corner to run for another block. It kept those inside secure, along with the cameras dotting the corners, watching every edge. Interestingly enough, he caught a glimpse of a tree, its branch hovering over the wall. Greenery in the city was becoming more common as people made an effort to have nature around them.

He really wished they'd stick to plastic. He was allergic to pollen and grass.

Following the length of the wall, Theodore reached a large gated driveway, wide enough for two vehicles at once. Approaching the closed gates, he noticed the intercom and the button below it. He pressed it with a handkerchief.

Bzzzzt.

Nothing happened.

"Excuse me?" He didn't know if anyone listened. "Hello?" He pressed the button again.

A tinny voice said drowsily, "What do you want?"

"I have an appointment with someone in unit five C."

"Come back another day."

"My appointment with her is today," Theodore insisted.

"It's fashionable to be late."

"Not for work it isn't." He fought to keep his cool. Why was the man on the intercom being so difficult?

"Whatever. If you're just going to whine about it, then come in."

With a click, a smaller door within the gate popped open, and Theodore stepped through, noticing the camera that watched him. The security wasn't too surprising. In the heart of the city, crime flourished. The residents of this condominium obviously valued privacy and safety.

It also had a surprising amount of greenspace. Theodore paused halfway to the massive condo building. While the driveway cut a dark swath that formed a roundabout at the front doors and also veered off to the right to an underground garage, the rest of the place was green. From the fence to the structure itself, bushes and trees flourished. People lay on the verdant grass, faces tilted to the warm sun.

The lazy indolence made him uncomfortable. Theodore was happiest at work. When he ran out of work to do, he found other things like cleaning, sorting his clothes by style and color, or rearranging his cabinets for maximum efficiency. He only spent one hour a day reading as his treat. His last girlfriend called him rigid and boring. He was all right with that. Although, with more than ten years passed since they'd broken up, might be time to revise his requirements in a partner.

As Theodore neared the building, he noticed the edges of a gate peeking above the door. It probably dropped down to cover the glass entrance. Interesting security feature.

The cameras by the door were obvious. The video eyes saw everything. He chose to ignore them.

Made of glass and trimmed in golden metal, the door slid open at his approach. That might have seemed like a lack of security until he caught sight of the beefy security guard behind a desk, who immediately zoned in on him. Theodore would have to check in.

Off to the side of the entrance, there were couches and some wide comfy chairs. A surprising amount of people lounged there. Mostly women. All quietly staring. Not saying a word. Kind of eerie.

For some reason he got an odd chill when one of them winked and smiled.

"Can I help you?" the guard asked. His nametag read Garfield.

"Hello, I'm Theodore Loomer from the IRS." He reached for his wallet, and the guard stood.

"Hands where I can see them," the guard barked, proving he wasn't as indolent as he first appeared.

"Just getting my identification." Theodore dropped the wallet open, flashing the badge.

The guard relaxed. "The IRS, eh? Here to see who?"

He pulled out a copy of the letter sent to the first name on his list. "Melly Goldeneyes."

"Ooooh, Melly's in trouble," someone shout-whispered behind him.

He turned, and every single person appeared busy and looking elsewhere.

The guard handed back the letter. "You'll want the fifth floor. Stairs or elevator?" The guard pointed in two directions.

"Aren't you going to buzz her?" he asked.

"And ruin the surprise?" Garfield smiled. It should have reassured, but it held a hint of smugness.

"Er, thank you." Clutching his briefcase, Theodore headed for the elevators, keeping an eye on the lounging people. While they seemed to ignore him, he couldn't help but feel at the same time they watched him intently. His skin prickled with awareness, and the urge to turn around for a peek meant he gritted his teeth and forged ahead.

The elevator already sat with the door open.

Theodore entered, pressed five, and turned around. As the doors closed, he was struck by the sudden turn of all the heads to peer in his direction. He could have sworn he heard laughter.

The interior of the cab, like the rest of the condo, was lavish, done in hues of gold with mirrors. His nose twitched. Somebody must have brought their damned pet with them. He could tell by his sudden urge to sneeze.

He put a handkerchief to his mouth.

The elevator spilled him onto the fifth floor just as it hit him.

Achoo.

As he recovered, he heard a door slam shut. Odd, he'd not seen anyone. A glance around showed a gray corridor—slate-colored carpet, pale walls, gold sconces to light the way.

Grip tight on his briefcase, he strode down the short hall to the T intersection. Left or right?

A glance on either side showed odd numbers to his left, even to his right. The doors were simple, and while they lacked a glass eye for peeping, he noted the cameras that watched his every move.

How much must a place like this cost given the amenities so far? How did the people he'd been sent to investigate afford it?

He chose a direction and his steps only slowed as he reached an open door. Music spilled out of it. A peek inside showed chaos.

So much chaos. Enough he yearned to grab a broom and sweep a clear path.

His nose wobbled again with an itch. Whoever lived here had a cat or a dog. Maybe both. This might get ugly. Hopefully he could do this interview quick.

He knocked lightly on the open portal.

No one replied.

"Hello?" he called, but the music masked his presence and he wasn't about to shout over it.

He stepped over the threshold and glanced around. A basic layout. Living room combined with dining and kitchen. A large window at the far end provided natural light. He noted the couch with its cushions on the floor, which made his left shoulder lift and lock. What kind of slob lived here?

The owner of the kitchen had decided to use the counter as a pantry with several open cereal boxes marching along, a bowl of fruit big enough to feed a family, and dishes in the sink.

His other shoulder tried to hunch. This mess wasn't his problem.

He took in more details, from the pizza box on what might be a coffee table—hard to tell with the bottles, cans, and game remotes covering it.

The televisions took up an entire wall. A big central flat screen flanked by four smaller ones. There were doors on the other half of the apartment. The one closest to where he stood was probably a closet. The one with clothes spilling out of it possibly the laundry. So much laundry.

Stepping carefully, he made his way through the tornado-stricken apartment. Surely the owner was here given the open door. He narrowly avoided stepping on a thong. A tiny scrap of light blue lace fabric.

The tickle grew stronger, and yet the place didn't smell. Not badly at least. Something scented the air, rather pleasant actually.

He moved past the underpants and the torn open box of snack cakes to the door past the horrifying laundry. He found the bouncing ass when he glanced through the next door.

A nice ass.

He remembered the driver's license picture.

"Ahem."

Head down, ass in the air, scrabbling for the sticky note that had fallen out of the sheaf of papers in her hand, the woman peeked between her legs, upside down. Her hair was a dark skein that tumbled, her eyes rimmed in thick lashes, and her brows nicely defined.

She eyed him. Probably admired the fine crease of his slacks compared to her rather ratty attire. Her jeans needed to be replaced given the number of holes.

"Who let you in?" she asked, still not straightening. Part of her buttocks peeked from the slit across it. Her panties, like the one pair he'd seen, were obviously not full bottomed.

If she wore any.

He looked away. "The door was wide open, and no one answered when I called out."

"Are you the IRS fellow?" she asked, reaching for

another sticky note on the sole of her shoe. Retrieving it, she unfolded herself—though not very far, as she only stood just over five feet—and looked up at him.

She was tiny. Tight. And somehow in his space. His bubble. He took a step back. "Are you Melly Goldeneyes?"

"Depends on who's looking."

"I'm from the IRS."

"According to my letter, you're early."

He tapped his watch. "Two p.m. on the nose."

"Haven't you heard of being fashionably late?"

"We have an appointment."

"I know, which is why I was organizing my stuff." She swept a hand to show all kinds of paper spread on the bed. "Tada!"

He glanced at the pile then her. "You can't be serious. That's not organized."

"Are you sure? Because it's all in one place."

He resisted the urge to shove at his glasses. The tickle in his nose got stronger. "Please gather them and bring them somewhere we can sort through them properly."

"Now?" she asked.

"Yes, now."

Her lips turned down. "But I was going to play soccer on the roof."

"Not until we've completed our business."

She sighed. "Can't we just get this over with? Yeah, I might have been a little creative with the stuff I claimed, but even Arik says my role is hard to define."

"Who is Arik?" Her boyfriend? Keeper? Someone who needed to hire this woman a maid?

"Arik's the boss."

"He employs you." He pulled out the file and flipped to the page. "Pride Industries. Family owned and operated."

"Not just family, or that'd be incest." Her nose wrinkled. "We're careful about those kinds of things." She eyed him up and down. "How's the genetics in your family?"

"None of your business," was his tart reply.

"Feisty. I like it." She flopped on the bed. "Shall we skip the small talk and go straight to the sex?"

"Excuse me?" His finger went to his tie as it constricted him. Sweat formed on his brow. This woman wasn't acting as expected.

"Please. I know how this works. I was a bad, bad girl and you want to help me with my problem. We both know you're waiting for me to bribe you to make this little IRS thing go away."

"You can't buy me off," he said tightly.

"Well, duh. I don't have any money, meaning sex is the obvious and, might I add, your best choice." She winked. "Don't worry, nerd boy. I am going to rock your world."

She went to touch him, and he recoiled, fast enough he hit the wall. "We are not having sex."

"Why not?" she huffed. "Don't tell me you're married. Do you have a girlfriend? You must. Only a jealous biatch would have you dressed like an uptight yuppie. I mean look at how straight that tie is." Once more she reached.

Again, he dodged. "Don't touch me."

"What's wrong? Afraid wifey poo will find out? You can shower when we're done. She'll never know. Although she might wonder why you have suddenly become a tiger in bed. Which is why I should probably warn you that sex with me will ruin you for other women."

"I am not married, and we are not having sex." The nerve of her. Bribing him with sex rather than admit she lied on her taxes.

Look at him saying no. Being morally superior to most people meant he didn't get laid often.

"No sex. Gotcha. In these times, gotta be careful. All kinds of diseases running rampant, but I assure you I am clean. But if you don't want to take my word for it, then I guess I can offer you a blowie."

"No."

"Two blowies and a finger in your bum?"

His cheeks clenched. "Ms. Goldeneyes, this is most annoying. I am not here to play games with you."

"That's a shame." She rolled on the papers. "I like games. Especially when I get to slap stuff around. Do you like to be slapped?" She batted her lashes.

He'd never been more tempted to crack his hand on someone's backside. Instead he straightened his spine and said in his sternest voice, "Gather the receipts and bring them to the kitchen table. We will work there."

"You wanna do it on the table? Kinky. I like it. Are we going to pull a retro nine and a half weeks and incorporate the fridge? I think I've got a can of whipped cream and some butter in there."

"Mold, too, I imagine," he muttered.

"Yeah, I wouldn't go near the cheese. I'm pretty sure it's spawned little curds and they're about to take over the entire dairy drawer."

His nose wobbled as it itched. "Do you have a cat?"

Her lips stretched into a wide smile. "As a matter of fact, I do. A big pussy. But she's nice when you get to know her. Pet her just right and she might even scratch."

"Isn't that purr?" he muttered, doing his best to keep his gaze off the woman sprawled on the bed, but then that meant seeing various lingerie strewn over the room and imagining her wearing it.

"Naw, when my pussy is happy, she yowls and bites." She winked. "Wanna meet her?"

His mind kept straying into the gutter, which might have been why he was rather terse as he said, "Bring the receipts to the table and keep your feline locked up. I'm not in the mood to pet any pussies today."

CHAPTER TWO

How fascinating. Mr. Prim and Proper walked away, and Melly wanted to know why. Was it that he didn't like women?

He'd certainly noticed her. She wasn't blind. He was attracted to her. She could smell it in the air.

Was he playing hard to get?

She did so love a challenge.

Could be she wasn't his type. Which would suck because he was very much her type. A hot geek in a suit begging to be peeled, with an impeccably tied cravat and thick-rimmed glasses she wanted to tear off. The IRS had sent her a hot nerd.

I could totally see myself doing numbers with him. All night long. Rowr.

"Excuse me?" he said, having obviously heard something. He glanced over his shoulder. She smiled wickedly.

He quickly turned away and seated himself at her

table. He shoved crap aside to have a clear spot to put his briefcase down.

He clicked it open. She kind of hoped to see a treasure trove. Maybe some dildos, nipple clamps restraints. To her disappointment, it was filled with paper.

He pulled forth a folder and closed the case of broken dreams. Setting it on the floor, he then put what she assumed to be her file down.

"Shall we begin?" he asked.

Curiosity drew her closer, and she jabbed a finger at the folder. "What's that?"

"Your dossier."

"What's it say?"

He bent down to rummage in his briefcase as he replied, "That you need to show me your receipts that we might discuss them."

Talk about uptight. She should offer to send him nudies. The poor man looked like he needed to tug a few off to relax.

The poor human was much too rigid. She didn't need her nose to realize she dealt with a human because a shifter male, upon seeing her tits down, ass up, would have done something dirty like slap her ass or hump it. He probably would have suffered a maiming as well—she chose whom she took to bed.

Upon seeing Mr. Hot Nerd, she'd been prepared to tear off his clothes, thinking she could kill two birds with one stone—remove the IRS threat and get shagged.

But he said no.

Her ego demanded a retry. But first...she swept the table clean.

The man cringed as the stuff hit the floor. "Would it have been so hard to put those things away?"

She blinked at him. "Away where?"

He poked in the direction. "Clothes in the laundry. Dishes in the kitchen."

"And have the maid think I don't need her? I couldn't do that to her." She shook her head.

"You have a maid?" The glance he tossed around the room appeared skeptical.

"She comes once a week. She says I'm her best client. I keep her busy," she confided.

"I'll bet," he muttered. "And are her wages part of your receipts?"

"Of course not," she hotly replied. "Cleaning is not work-related unless I have a home office. Even I know that."

"I'm glad you understand the difference. Now if you don't mind"—he tapped the table—"the receipts."

He was so cute when he was forceful, with his dark hair cut in perfect short lines. His lips could use a good chewing.

Only he'd said no.

The nerve.

Given he wouldn't budge, she hit her bedroom and emerged with an armful of receipts and paper. She dumped it on the table, some of it fluttering and slipping off before she sat across from him.

"Tada."

He looked positively dumbstruck. He probably didn't often have people like her who obeyed him. To think, people were scared of the IRS. She planned to cooperate and make this easy on him. Maybe then she'd get to take off that tie, or at the very least bat it.

He snared a thin sheet of paper and frowned. "This bill is for this current year. I only want the ones applying to last year's taxes."

"They're in there, too, along with the year before that."

"You mean, all of this…" He didn't sigh. She could tell he wanted to, but he held himself back.

Could she push him over that edge? "I like to keep them all in a drawer in my bedroom. Except now it's mostly the dresser on account I haven't sorted it out in a while." Surely, he'd snap.

"For future reference, you should separate them by year and type," he stated, pulling at some of them, creating piles.

"That sounds long and boring." Hypnotic though. She watched his hands, eyes bouncing, feeling her ass wiggling in the seat, wanting to pounce.

"Being organized will help you conform to the law."

He probably wouldn't appreciate her thoughts on laws, so she leaned forward on her elbows and stared at him instead. "Do you have a name?"

"Theodore Loomer."

"Such a serious name," she teased. "You seem more like a Theo."

"You may address me as either Theodore or Mr. Loomer."

"Mr. Loomer. Sounds like something I'd call a teacher." She winked. "I like it. Would my teacher like to give me a hands-on lesson?"

If she hadn't watched, she might not have seen the flare of his nostrils.

"If we might return to the business at hand. Shall we discuss your tax return?"

"I'd rather discuss you. Why the Internal Revenue Service? Do you like being hated? Is it a fetish for you?"

A tic along his jaw brought a smile to her lips.

"I'm good with numbers."

"I'll bet that's not all you're good at," she purred.

Still watching him, she didn't miss the subtle shifting of his body. Theodore might be saying no, but the man proved very much aware.

"Let's start with the basics. Name and date of birth."

"Aren't they on the paper in front of you?" She leaned over the table and pointed.

"It was for confirmation."

"You're in my apartment. How much more confirmation do you need?"

"Are you Melly Goldeneyes?"

"Yes."

"Short for anything?"

"Just Melly. My mother doesn't believe in middle names or fancy ones."

"Date of birth."

"A lady never tells." She snickered. "But we both know I'm not a lady. I'm July thirty-first, nineteen ninety something."

He looked at her.

She shrugged. "Mama isn't too sure what year I was born. She had me in the woods and lost track of time."

"It says ninety-five." He jabbed with his pen.

"Sure. Let's go with that."

He sighed, and she counted it as a small victory. "Marital status?"

"Single but seeking. Not having much luck though. I tried that app where you swipe left or right depending on if you're interested. But most of those guys are looking for one-night stands, and I'm not into that. I think sex should have meaning."

He snorted. "Ironic you should say that given you offered it to me not ten minutes ago."

"Sex to clear my good tax name would have had meaning, not to mention I probably would have found god or some other deity when you were inside me."

He definitely trembled.

She smirked. "But you said no." Perkily spoken. "Why did you say no? Should I call in my cousin Bertrand to handle you? He's about my age and packs about nine inches—"

He cut her off. "For the last time, I am not interested in sex with you or anyone."

"Well, you don't have to be rude about it." She might have been a bit sassy in her reply, mostly because he could deny all he wanted. She knew he lied.

"Can we get back to your return?"

"If we must." She leaned back in her chair and balanced it on two legs.

"You claimed an income of eighty-three thousand last year."

"I did."

"With expenses of seventy-four."

"And?"

"That's almost your entire income."

"Again, and?"

"It's impossible. Your condo mortgage and fees alone would be at least a third."

"I have no mortgage."

He glanced at her. "You own this apartment?"

"Not exactly. The family loans it to me. Free of charge."

"Even if it's paid for, there are other expenses. Phone, food, insurance."

"All covered for me by the company."

"The Pride Group pays for those things?" He sounded surprised.

"Everyone who lives in the condo gets it all-inclusive. We're pretty lucky here. Arik's been amazing." She was babbling, and he took notes.

"That seems rather generous."

"What can I say? Arik is considered a king amongst his family." In more ways than one.

"What exactly is your job within the company?"

She straightened in her seat. "Whatever he needs. When lucky, I get security detail."

"You?" He eyed her for longer than he had previously.

She made sure to breathe deep and stick out her chest. "You don't have to be big to be mighty. I'm more of an inside-job kind of person."

"Security from what?"

"The rats in the business." Mr. Hot Nerd Loomer didn't need to know the rats were literal. But their hacking skills weren't anywhere to being on par with hers.

He reached for a paper near the piles he'd started and eyed it. "Can you explain what this receipt is for?"

He, of course, pointed out the biggest one. His eyes serious behind his glasses.

"That's for ten thousand rounds of ammunition." Blame his cuteness for the distraction that had her blurting the truth rather than the lie she'd been practicing.

"Ammo." He stared at the bill. "Ammo for what?"

"Target practice. I've been improving my aim so I'm not always stuck working in the office. I get stuck with so many keyboard jobs, it's not funny."

For a second his lips parted, and he murmured, "I know the feeling."

"Anyhow, I figure if I can shoot the eye out of a turkey running full tilt at fifty yards, I can do anything. Which is why the fee for the range is also in the pile there somewhere. I have an annual membership." She rifled through the sheets.

"If it's a hobby, you can't claim it."

"I never said it was a hobby." She took the upgrade of her skills seriously. She wanted to branch out from the hacking to fieldwork.

He snared another bill and waved it. "What about this receipt? What's it for?"

"Rocket launcher."

He paused before saying, "Why would you need a rocket launcher?"

"Because it's fun?"

"Exactly what do you fire at?"

"Mostly just targets. I've been practicing since you never know when I might have to shoot a helicopter out of the sky in the name of duty."

"That kind of thing only happens in the movies."

"If you say so." No need to divulge they had an excellent scrubbing team whose only job was to keep their secrets and wipe away any crimes—or overeager protection of the pride. Not a single online trace remained about the run of the lions down Fifth Street. The magic mushrooms used in the gravy drizzled over the roast beef dinner at Thanksgiving took a few hours to wear off.

"I do say so. And I also think you're lying. This isn't for ammunition and artillery."

"Believe me or not, I told you what it is. Up to you how you handle it."

"How about I reject it as being unsuitable?"

"Ouch, that's kind of harsh. You'll hurt the poor things' feelings." She cradled the receipt for the flamethrower she'd just had to have.

He didn't laugh. How far was that stick up his ass?

"Not acceptable. Not acceptable." He began slamming receipts aside in an increasing stack.

She took offense. "Hey, you're rejecting everything."

"Because they're all inadmissible. This is for personal care. You can't claim it." He waved the pink sheets for the mani/pedis she got every month.

"I disagree. How am I supposed to do my job if my claws aren't sharp?"

He eyed her fingers and the coral polish on them. "I highly doubt you're clawing people in the line of duty."

"I hope that wasn't meant to be sexist."

He eyed her. "I'm quite certain you are perfectly capable of defending yourself."

"I most certainly can, although if I had a man to call my own, I'd save all the biting and scratching for him." She winked as suggestively as she could.

He completely ignored it. "You can't claim your manicures."

"What if I argued firing that many rounds is hell on the hands?"

He glared. He almost got kissed it was so adorable. The man was utterly fascinating.

"I still fail to see how firing weapons ties into your employment."

"It's on account I do security."

"No, you don't. On here, you're marked as restaurant hostess." He pointed to a copy of the tax documents she'd sent in.

"Okay, so maybe the security part isn't full time yet." Barely even part time, given Arik tended to give the juicy jobs to the more experienced in the pride. "A girl needs to be ready. Do you know how many movies I've seen where the waitress is taken out first? Screw that. I keep a semi-automatic tucked under one of the tables. Anyone tries to *Die Hard* my office and I am going to kablam them!"

Rather than looked impressed, he made another note and the stack of receipts threatened to topple. "Personal care and ammo for hobbies are not allowable deductions."

"But they really are for work."

"Are you admitting you were paid for the security work but did not properly declare it?"

"I'm not sure what I'm saying, but if you're implying I have two jobs..." Her nose wrinkled. "Bad enough I've got to show up for the one. No way do I have two. Security is what I volunteer for to avoid a stint at the restaurant. I'm too pretty to be working inside." She tossed her dark hair, the envy of her friends who were all shades of blonde. She stood out and liked it that way.

"I know you're lying about not getting paid extra, because how else do you afford clothes and meals?"

"The Pride takes care of it."

He set his pen down to regard her seriously. "Miss Goldeneyes, if the company takes care of everything, then why give you a paycheck at all?"

"For fun of course." She knew her cheeks dimpled when she smiled.

Mr. Hot Geek noticed, too, and shoved at his glasses. "Aha, but you just said shooting was for work!"

"You caught me. So maybe the ammo isn't quite work related yet. Not a big deal, we'll take it off."

"It's not that simple."

"Sure, it is. I'm still willing to strike a deal. Three blowies, a cowgirl, and I'll let you stick your finger up my bum."

"No!" More scribbled notes.

"What if I said I'll be wearing my latex suit with cutouts in strategic spots?" she said, ending on sultry whisper.

"Ms. Goldeneyes, you're going to force me to file a sexual harassment complaint."

"Maybe I should file one given you're not giving me anything to work with." Her lower lip jutted.

"We have business to attend."

"What if you didn't and it was you and me meeting for the first time?"

"No."

"It's the zombie apocalypse and we're the only two living people."

"Zombies aren't real."

"Don't tell that to the Laveau chick visiting us. She won't shut up about her great-grandma something or other who was some witch."

"If you're referencing Madame Laveau, according to the stories, she was more than a voodoo queen but a necromancer of great renown. A necromancer—"

"Raises dead people." She rolled her eyes. "Hello. Girls play D&D games, too, you know."

"I don't."

"Play with games or girls?" she deliberately taunted.

"Let's return to the ammunition. Where did you get the ammo? The receipt only gives the stock number and quantity. There is no company name or address."

"Because Marney doesn't like to give receipts for goods."

"Who is Marney?"

"No one." She'd not meant to speak out loud or mention her supplier by name. Damn her tongue for getting away again. She would have to be more careful. The nerd was drawing things out of her she didn't mean to admit.

"No one sold you the ammunition?"

She wagged her finger at him. "You're tricky, Poindexter."

"Did you just insult me?"

"I called you smart, so not really. Next question."

His expression turned even stonier. "What kind of protection does Pride Industries require that you think you need training?"

A subtle question but she now paid attention. "You know how it is in the hair product world. Gnarly. Which is why he likes our security conditioned. Get it?"

Judging by his face, he didn't. "Given you're a waitress, eighty-three thousand dollars a year seems rather excessive."

"Only if you work at one of those fast food places. A Lion's Pride Steakhouse is a top-notch restaurant."

"It's a steakhouse." Her nerd almost sneered. How cute.

"Don't you like meat? I love meat. Chewing it. Playing with it. Hunting it down and pouncing on it." She batted her lashes and licked her lips in an attempt to distract, but he remained untouched.

Was she overdoing it? His human ass should have succumbed to her charm by now. Perhaps she was too far away from him. She had to get closer.

As she was halfway across the table, he exclaimed, "What are you doing?"

She glanced down. She might have forgotten herself for a moment there. Blame the nerd. He smelled good.

Real good. Lick him head to toe good. Drag him around in her mouth and growl at anyone who looked in her direction good.

"Just thought I'd get closer to help you sort through the stuff." She slunk into the chair beside him.

He shifted away from her.

Ah, how cute. She made the human nervous. He just didn't shake or stammer. Curious.

She leaned close and—

Achoo.

He sneezed. Hard.

"Do you have a cold?" she asked. Not that she cared. She had an iron constitution, but she wasn't about to deal with the snot that came out of humans when they got one.

"It's my allergies. Probably the cat you mentioned."

"Allergic to cats. This is priceless." she said with a snicker. "Especially given my big, hairy pussy likes to roll around and shed fur on all the furniture."

He looked absolutely appalled. "How can you let it do that? I don't understand."

"Understand what?"

"How can you want some smelly, hairy creature in your things? Lap. Nothing would ever be clean."

"Is cleanliness important to you, Theo?" she purred, leaning close.

"Yes, as is doing my job." He spilled out of his seat. "Given you're not ready for me, I'm going to return at a later date."

"When?"

"I have a meeting tomorrow with someone else in the building. Perhaps after?"

"Who?" she snarled, only to quickly smile. "I mean, what are the chances more than one of us is undeserving of your attention?" Lashes batted.

He remained immune and wearing his pants. "Have all your receipts for last year in a pile. We'll review them tomorrow, say around three?"

She shook her head. "That will never do. Tonight. Seven o'clock. Meet me at the steakhouse you just disparaged."

"A restaurant is hardly the proper place to sort these things."

"We're going because I need food, you need food, and the next time you say steakhouse it should be with a happy lilt. Not to mention, you might possibly understand why I needed those brass knuckles for my job as hostess."

"You claimed brass knuckles?" He cast a side-eye at the pile of receipts they'd yet to look at.

"Well, they call them that, but really, the metal is more like an alloy. I can't pronounce some of the stuff it uses, but it's solid. Nothing but the best for my work."

"You need an accountant."

"Funny you should say that because the one I used to have said I needed a keeper." It might be why she had to get a new accountant. Given she hacked computers for fun, it wasn't hard to figure out a way to have her stuff automatically sorted and filed using the fund transfers from her various accounts. But her programming let her down by not distinguishing hidden purchases from real ones. She'd had to scramble to find the actual paper for more than a few things the program claimed. In some cases, she improvised.

Some might wonder why she didn't hack the IRS and clear her name. She could, it wasn't that hard, and she was pretty good at not getting caught. Most of the time. She well remembered the punishment when Arik found out she'd been playing with the government's airspace defense system. All she did was set off a few missiles for some real fireworks. Not a big deal. Arik laid down his paw and relegated her to latrine duty; AKA cleaning the public toilets on the condo's ground floor. It still gave her nightmares.

"Perhaps you should have listened to them, because you obviously don't know how to care for yourself." He eyed her place with clear disparagement as he stood and weaved gingerly to the door.

The discomfort in him made her want to lick him and see what happened next. Would he scream like a baby? Run for the nearest shower and soap? Turn into a passionate beast who pinned her to the wall?

"I can't wait to have you discipline me over dinner," she declared as he headed out the door.

"Have your papers ready," was his dry reply as he left, closing the door behind him.

She ran for the security panel and flipped it on for a peek, pushing the button marked Hall. Without pausing that long stride, he turned down the hall for the elevator. Would he actually leave? She ran for the remotes scattered in the living room. Diving on the tablet poking out from under a cushion, she quickly loaded her menu options. The security camera footage of the lobby loaded, four in all: one by the elevator, one each by the desk and lounge, the last by the front door.

She watched Mr. Theodore Loomer leaving, posture tall, his head never turning to look, meaning he never saw the women perched on the edges of their seats, watching him.

Only once Melly knew he was gone did she flounce downstairs into the main lobby, receiving instant silence as she announced, "Biatches, we have a problem."

CHAPTER THREE

There was a problem. Despite his mandate to uncover financials and the threads that would lead from them, Theodore found himself outside the steakhouse at six fifty-five. A habit of his was arriving a few minutes early that he might check things out.

A Lion's Pride Steakhouse was a well-known eatery owned, no surprise, by the Pride Group—who also made their money in luxury hotels and hair products, of all things. Yet they seemed a little too successful. Given some of the things he'd gleaned from the files, he knew for a fact they had to be dealing in some shady stuff, too. If he could ferret out the secret, he'd be in for a promotion and a raise.

There were a few ways he could tackle this. There was the actual tax fraud angle, which was the most obvious easiest. The ammo itself was black market stuff, and thus no taxes had been paid. And then there was whatever the Pride Group was hiding. It must be big given Melly Goldeneyes appeared quite earnest when she claimed she'd been training and accumulating weaponry for work.

Brass knuckles. How did a pretty and petite thing like her expect him to believe she fought bare knuckles?

And what kind of employee thought she needed to shoot down helicopters to do her job?

The hum of an engine had him eyeing askance the single light bearing down on him. The motorcycle screamed to a stop and he knew who sat on the seat straddling the big motor.

"Theo! There you are, and right on time, too, I'll bet." She swung a leg off the bike and peeled off her pink glitter helmet. She shook out her dark hair. The leather jacket and jeans she wore were form fitting. The toes of her boots scuffed.

They couldn't have looked more mismatched. "Evening, Ms. Goldeneyes."

"So formal, Theo. Call me Melly. Just don't call me your sexy bitch, or I will jump you. In a dirty good way of course." She winked.

He tried to steer her in a better direction. "Do you have the paperwork I requested in order?"

"Nope."

"Why not?"

"Because you're just going to tell me I can't claim any of it, so what's the point?"

"The point is without those deductions you'll owe thousands."

"Yada. Yada. We'll discuss business later," she said. "Ready for the best steak of your life?"

He'd not meant to eat. He'd planned to get her to hand over the stuff. Then, as she claimed, reject them, thus giving her the choice of paying for her crime or rolling on someone else.

Instead, when she grabbed his hand, he followed docilely as she led him inside. She never looked before she tossed her helmet at the podium, yelling, "Heads up, Clara."

Clara gave her the finger with one hand and caught the helmet with the other.

Melly didn't wait to be seated but led him away from a dining room half full of diners to an even bigger one past some swinging doors. Rowdier, too, until they walked in. Too many sets of eyes zeroed in on him. Was it him, or did a few of them glow golden?

Melly waved. "Hey, biatches. This is my new friend Theo, the IRS guy I was telling you about."

A good chunk of the room suddenly evaporated. He blinked, and bam, they were gone. He'd never get used to the irrational fear people had of someone who worked for the Treasury Department. Obey the laws, file the paperwork, and pay the correct amount of tax. How hard could it be?

Hard enough there was no shortage of investigations.

Melly didn't seem perturbed one bit that her choice to bring him had caused half the place to clear out. She grabbed him by the hand and dragged him to a recently vacated table in the middle of the room.

Immediately he began to itch. His nose also began to twitch. Did they let animals inside the restaurant? Someone should call the health inspector on them.

Before he could sneeze, Melly shoved something at him. A little pink pill.

He waved a hand and his head. "I don't do drugs."

"It's for your allergies."

"I'm fine."

"Please. Your eyes are getting ready to water, and you look like you're about to bust a lung sneezing."

"I am not taking medication from you."

"Why not?"

"Because."

Her lips curved. "You mean you don't trust me. Smart man. But here's the thing. If I wanted to drug your ass, I wouldn't make it obvious. I'd slip something into your water. Or food."

"I'll remember that."

"I also wouldn't waste any of my happy drugs on someone who wouldn't appreciate them."

"You use drugs?"

"Sometimes, but only if it's safe. Arik's got rules about us losing control in public. Social media ruins all our fun." Her lips turned down.

"Thanks, but no thanks." He handed the pill back, and his hand brushed hers. A shock went through him, and his startled gaze met hers.

Someone in the room gagged.

The moment ended. He sat down, briefcase on the floor. "If you've decided not to claim anything, then there's really no need for this meeting." He'd move onto the next person on his list. Maybe they'd be easier to crack.

"Well, you've got me all worried now about what I can claim. You're saying no to all the best stuff. Bet you're going to tell me next bullet-making classes don't count under education."

He resisted an urge to remove his glasses and pinch the bridge of his nose. She did it on purpose. Totally on purpose. Being ridiculous in the hopes he'd just go away. But he couldn't leave. He eyed her. "This isn't funny."

"Never said it was."

"You have all kinds of things on here that don't make sense. "Bullet-making is not an acceptable educational choice."

"Even if it saves the company money?" she countered.

"Does Pride Industries make ammunition?"

"No." And he could just tell by her expression that she wished they did.

Such a strange woman.

"Given it doesn't relate to your employment, and is a hobby, you can't use it as a deduction."

"Figures. All the things to help me survive the zombie apocalypse are being repressed by the government. I swear, it's like they're doing it on purpose.

Don't let us learn how to defend ourselves, taking away our guns."

"You can learn to shoot, you just can't ask for a rebate on your taxes for it."

"Fine," she huffed. "Mind not telling anyone though? I'm already going to be in trouble. I mean when Arik finds out we didn't use an accountant to file our taxes, he's gonna murder us." She dragged a finger over her throat.

Instantly, his focus changed. "Are you worried he'll harm you?"

"As if Arik would hurt me." She laughed so hard she almost fell out of her chair.

"A 'no' would have sufficed," Theodore said stiffly.

"But you're so cute when you're silly."

The insult bound in a compliment warmed and annoyed at once. "I am assuming from your own statement that your employer is unaware of the tax fraud you perpetrated."

"Say nothing, Melly." A woman sprawled over the booth and smiled at him. Her tawny skin was offset by golden hair and vivid green eyes.

"Excuse me?" Theodore frowned at the woman rudely interrupting. She didn't seem daunted at all as she slid into the seat beside Melly.

"Did you fart?" the stranger asked.

He gaped and sputtered. "No."

"Didn't think so. I would have smelled it. So why are you apologizing?"

"I was actually trying to politely comment on your

rude interruption of our discussion." Theo's stick rammed him straight in the seat.

"No discussion because Melly knows better than to talk about Pride business to outsiders. Right?" The green gaze zeroed in on Melly, who didn't seem daunted in the least.

"He's with the IRS."

"Blood-sucking vulture," the woman muttered.

"Ignore Zena," Melly said to him. "She's antiestablishment."

"And I am also the Pride's top lawyer, meaning if you want to ask Melly questions, they go through me."

"She isn't under arrest," was his stiff reply.

"Does this mean no handcuffs later?" Melly winked.

Given the image he suddenly had involved cuffs, Melly, and no clothes, he was happy the tablecloth fell partially over his lap. "Meeting here wasn't a good idea. We should reschedule."

"Don't leave." Melly reached out, leaning over the table to do so, and grabbed his hand.

He looked down at her fingers on him, the skin of hers calloused compared to the softer skin on his. But that surely wasn't the reason he felt a thrill every time she touched him. "We aren't getting anything done."

"Good. Keep it that way," the lawyer snapped.

"You can't tell me what to do," Melly said.

"Actually, I can. Conditions of your contract and all." Zena smirked. "But never fear, I'll handle this fine government agent."

"Paws off, Zena," Melly growled. "I saw him first."

"Don't make me tell your mother."

Theodore ping-ponged his attention between the women.

"Tell her what, that I'm having dinner with a guy? Go right ahead," Melly sassed. "She keeps bugging me to settle down and make some cubs for her to spoil."

"So long as it's not with him." Zena slewed him an unimpressed look before slinking away.

He felt the need to reiterate two things, "We won't be having sex, and there's no need for a lawyer yet. I'm sure we can come to an arrangement."

"An arrangement with no sex. I'm intrigued. But later. Business can wait. Let's eat."

Despite not having ordered, a plate layered with crispy calamari rings arrived as she spoke. It wouldn't hurt to have a few bites.

An hour later, he was groaning and Melly was still eating. He'd only managed one piece of the dessert before he gladly gave her the rest. She ate it, plus the sixteen-ounce steak, the potato, the salad, the fried mushrooms. He'd never seen a woman with a healthier appetite.

Never known anyone so vivacious and bubbly. She might act dumb, but she was a lot smarter than she let on. He wondered how much of the bubbly-airhead thing was an act.

Melly leaned back, patted her belly, and said, "Thank gawd I wore my stretchy jeans. Teach me to have a snack before dinner."

"What did you have?"

"Two burgers and a shake."

"That's a meal."

"No, a meal has fries," she corrected.

"How do you eat like that and remain..." He paused before saying sexy. "Trim?"

"I have a good metabolism." She winked. "What do you do to work out?"

He shrugged. "This and that." Of late, since he'd been assigned new tasks, he'd not had as much time as he'd like to work out.

As they ate, the initial crowd that had disappeared at the announcement of the IRS in their midst returned, their conversations a hum of background noise. The gazes only straying every so often with curiosity.

Theodore had allowed himself to relax. His guard came down. But it was past time he did the job he'd been tasked with.

Just as she placed her lips around the last piece of cake, the door to the dining room was thrust open and a loud voice shouted, "Don't try anything funny or we'll shoot."

As if to make his point, the leader of the invading force brandished a weapon.

Melly uttered an "uh-oh."

And Theodore went into an epic sneezing fit.

CHAPTER FOUR

A good thing Theo had sneezed and buried his face in a napkin or he might have noticed the gunmen weren't one hundred percent human. Damn those dumb city bears. Get them a little excited and out popped their grizzly side.

What were they thinking, busting into the place without checking for humans first? It was a wonder they hadn't been outed.

Theo was still recovering from his sneezing fit. Without thinking twice, Melly reached out and knocked the glasses off his face. "Oops. Sorry about that."

Not really, though. The less he could see, the better. She'd hate to have to explain to a human how bears ended up in a restaurant. Then there was the fact he seemed the type to call in health inspectors.

Her background search on him had pegged him as exactly what he seemed: a straight geek who'd graduated with honors, done a few months in the military, washed out, and ended up getting hired by the Internal Revenue Service.

No girlfriend. No wife. No living family. Not even a damned fish in a bowl. The man was a loner through and through.

And he fascinated her.

He looked utterly adorable, blinking those eyes, gazing around with a crease on his brow. "What's happening?"

"No idea," she lied and then didn't have to say more, as Theo once more went off in a sneezing fit.

"Everyone, stop what you're doing!" shouted the grizzly leading the sleuth of bears. "And listen up."

She had chosen a fine night to take Theo out, having forgotten that, with the changing of the leaves, the annual football game was imminent. Bears versus lions. It was a rough-and-tumble match that ended in bruises, swearing, sweat, and dirt. Also barbecued ribs, chicken, a few roasted pigs over spits, the most corn ever seen cooked in one spot, and more pies than could be counted on fingers and toes. Mouthwatering—

"Would you stop it already? No one can hear me over your sneezing." A hand—just barely keeping its human shape—went to slam the table.

Given Theo had his face buried in a napkin, dying of allergies, she snared the almost paw and tsked. "Now, now, Percy, no need to be rude."

"Your boyfriend is ruining the moment," grumbled

Percy. "Do you know how long I've been practicing my speech?"

"A whole day?" she wagered.

Every year, the sleuth chose someone to head the challenge, and every year, that bear, rather than planning something truly epic, jumped to extend the challenge prematurely.

"Almost two," Percy whined.

"Achoo."

"What the hell is wrong with him?" Percy jerked his head at Theo.

"He's allergic," she explained since it wasn't obvious to the big meathead.

"To what?" Percy asked.

"Cats for starters." Although she was beginning to think he was more allergic to bears.

Her reply, of course, caused Percy to laugh. The kind of laugh that had him leaning on the table, almost wiping tears, dying of humor.

"Guess he's not much of a boyfriend," Percy said with a snicker.

The big dumb jerk. In normal circumstances, she'd have wiped that smirk off his face. Something in her expression must have shown her violent need, because Percy recoiled. She made a mental note to play around in his bank account later. Maybe shut off his gaming accounts.

Theo chose that moment to finally stop his fit and lifted his face from his napkin. He appeared flushed and annoyed. His fault. He should have taken the pill.

Over the years, the shapeshifter community had developed some of the best allergy meds in the world. They didn't have a choice, given even humans with no allergies often reacted strongly to their presence.

Theo's myopic gaze narrowed in on Percy. How much could he see? The lenses in his glasses appeared thick. Was he nearsighted or far?

Whatever the case, his ears worked fine as he replied, "I am not her boyfriend."

Not surprisingly, Percy laughed louder. "I should hope not. She's a freaking man-eater. A real she-cat when it's that time of the month, liable to tear you a new one if you cross her, eh."

"Spoken by the big idiot standing within reach." A soft threat with a promising smile.

Percy paled under his tan and took a nervous step back. "Just some friendly ribbing."

"It's unwelcome. You need to go. Now," she added, in case it wasn't clear.

"But I'm not done. I haven't issued the challenge yet," he whined.

"What challenge?" Theo asked.

Before Percy could answer, someone else yelled, "We are here to challenge you mangy fucking felines to a duel to the death. An epic feat of prowess and speed where only the toughest will survive. Blood will be shed. Tears, too, as you lose. Are you ready to have your asses handed to you?" As announcements went, it was meant to be inciting.

She knew it. Percy knew it. But the idiot yelling

had yet to realize they had an unknowing human in their midst.

Melly snapped, "This is not the time to start trouble."

But the youth, probably influenced by the adrenaline of a coming fight, couldn't contain himself. "There is no better time to start trouble than now." He then lifted his gun and fired.

There could have been a herd of humans with cameras inside. It wouldn't have stopped the explosion of violence. The Pride had just been challenged. Only a coward wouldn't reply.

More of the weapons went off in a cacophony of noise, splats, and yodels. Butter knives and forks went flying. Scraps of clothes, too.

Ah hell.

Before Theodore could think to squint for a peek, she yanked her human geek under the table, hiding him behind the hanging tablecloth.

"What is going on?" he exclaimed, his head turned to the noise. He could hear, just not see, and what he heard surely had to cause him some anxiety. Screams. Growls. Things breaking.

Yet he didn't appear frightened. He crouched with her and stared intently at the tablecloth as if he could see through it. What plausible excuse could she have for the chaos?

"It's a neighborhood gang. Probably planning to shake the restaurant down."

"Seems more like Armageddon."

"I'm sure it sounds worse than it is. Stay here while I go for a peek." Melly went to crawl out from under the tablecloth but didn't get far. A firm grip around her ankle made sure of it.

"Where are you going?" Theo asked as the bears kept firing and someone—most likely Luna—screamed, "I am going to tear your face off and shove it up your anus for ruining my dinner."

She would. Almost ready to give birth, Luna got hangry when people interrupted her meal.

"It's okay," Melly soothed. "I'm going to check out what's happening."

His face took on a stubborn cast. "There's people shooting off guns. If anyone goes out to scout things, it should be me."

"Sexist much?" she asked.

"It has nothing to do with you being a woman but common courtesy. I did a few months in the military."

"You mean like the cadets?"

"No," was his terse reply. "I enlisted when I was eighteen."

"You?" Forget the fight. This was more interesting.

"Yes me."

"And washed out."

His jaw gritted. "As a matter of fact, I quit when they told me I'd never be able to do anything other than a desk job because of my eyesight."

"And then still got a desk job." She couldn't help but tease.

"Don't remind me," he muttered. "But the point is I have the training for these kinds of situations."

She almost patted his cheek at his brave yet misplaced bravado. "You're cute Poindexter, but you can't see a thing. Don't worry. I'll be fine. They wouldn't dare shoot me."

Except someone did. By accident, she should add. The moment she stood a missile hit her in the chest.

She glanced down at the dripping green paint. The bears dared attack with paintballs, and this after being told to never bring them inside again.

The bears weren't the only ones with missiles. The lions might not have paintballs, but they had food, and it went whipping through the air: baked potatoes fully loaded that hit and splattered, bowls of salad, even a piece of steak. That was a travesty.

The remains of dinner was fired at the bears, including Percy, who ducked, meaning the leftovers hit her full in the face.

The guttural word she uttered might not have been entirely ladylike. Her threat even less. "I am going to murder the lot of you."

Sure enough, the violent promise drew the attention of the man under the table. He went to crawl out, flipping the cloth back, about to stand. Even with his myopic gaze, he was bound to realize something was amiss.

She did the only thing she could.

She snared a nearby chair and clobbered him over the head, hard enough he fell, face down. He lay on the floor unmoving, and she bit her lip chagrinned. Had she hit him too hard? She didn't see any blood. Kneeling by his side, she flipped him over and pressed her fingers to his neck to check his pulse.

Some smartass decided to really push her last button. "Look at Melly. So desperate to get some she's got to knock her boyfriend out."

The idiot who opened his mouth got it stuffed with a few napkins and had to suffer the embarrassing haircut she gave him using only a steak knife.

Once that happened, the melee more or less ended. It hadn't lasted long, only the length of time needed for the dining room to become an utter dripping mess of paint and food. Lots of grinning faces, too.

Percy, the furry ass who started it all, had a shit-eating grin through the pasta sauce dripping from his beard. "That went better than expected. See you Sunday, eleven a.m. at the farm?"

"I say we start the party sooner. Shooters at The Claw!" shouted a lioness who liked to have a good time.

Usually Melly would have been leading the charge to the tavern up the street with its wide plank floors and paw-stomping music, but she had a responsibility to handle first.

Given Theo was a little heavier than expected, her friend Joan helped her carry him outside to her bike. It became quickly obvious that carrying him on it wouldn't work. He kept flopping over, his body a loose noodle.

"Just stick him in a cab," Joan suggested, an athletic woman in her early forties with a blonde bob, streaked with a bit of silver.

"We could use bungee cords to hold him on?" Luna—who had joined them outside, pregnant belly leading the way, eating a hunk of steak—suggested.

Melly actually considered it.

"Why not take his wheels?" Reba still looked immaculate, in spite of the fact Melly had seen her flinging food off her fork. Reba knelt in her heels and, in a moment, stood, Theo's wallet in one hand, keys in the other. "According to his very handy 'if lost, please return card,' he doesn't live too far."

"I could drive him home I guess, but what about my bike?" Melly couldn't exactly leave it at the restaurant.

"I'll drive it."

"No, me."

"It's my turn."

There wasn't a shortage of volunteers to make sure it got back to the condo. As a matter of fact, it was gone before she'd finished saying Luna's name.

She pouted at the receding taillight. "How am I supposed to get home?"

Arik had banned Melly from using any kind of ride sharing services. Even taxis were a no-no because of a few incidents. If the driver didn't want her to break his arm, he shouldn't stop the car in dark places and think he could grope her. He was lucky she didn't tear it off and beat him with it. She settled for having his licenses revoked and the parking enforcement, who had a sheaf of tickets in his name, given his location for an arrest.

"Please, as if you're coming home before morning," Joan stated.

The gang of lionesses in the alley with her outright laughed.

A good point.

"Want me to ride with you and give you a hand getting him to bed?" Joan offered.

"I'll be okay. I can handle him."

"I'll bet you can." Joan smirked. "He's pretty for a human. I can see why you like him."

Apparently, her friend had gotten the wrong impression. "It's not like that. You know he works for the IRS and he's digging into my taxes. I have to do something before he comes after us all."

"Look at you, taking one for the team. Much appreciated." Reba winked. "Have fun."

Fun? With an unconscious man? Tempting, but that was another no-no. All sexual partners of the human variety must be conscious, unbound, and not fearing for their lives.

"I say you snuggle him until he wakes up, and when he does and starts freaking out, tell him he's your husband and you've got like six kids." Joan had an evil sense of humor.

"Let's just find his car," Melly muttered.

They supported him, one under each arm, toting him along as if he were drunk. By following his scent, they found his vehicle parked not far away, a sensible four-door sedan in a dark gray. The interior was immaculate.

Even Reba looked impressed. "Not even a drop of coffee in the holders."

Not a speck of dust dared mar the dash, and the radio was on a respectable soft rock station. So boring. Poor Theo, he really needed to learn to let loose a little. He redefined the term uptight.

Rather than try and strap him upright to the passenger seat, they dumped him in the trunk. Joan tapped on the driver side window before Melly could pull out of the parking lot.

She rolled down the window. "What?"

Carla took on a serious mien. "This IRS fellow. You know what Arik will say."

Arik, being the king, wouldn't like it if there was even the slightest chance Theo had seen something.

"He wasn't wearing his glasses."

"Is he deaf or dumb?"

"No."

"Then chances are he noticed something."

"I'll convince him he dreamt it. After all, head injuries can cause delusions."

"And if he doesn't believe it?"

Melly took a moment to reply. "I know what I have to do."

Protect the pride at all cost.

It didn't take long to drive Theo's car to the address he'd programmed as home into his GPS. She parked the car on the street in front of a converted duplex. A quiet, rather boring façade on a boring street. He had a garage door opener clipped to the visor. A metal door ratcheted upwards.

The garage was ridiculous. Immaculate with recycling bins neatly lined. Tools neatly hung on a pegboard rather than lying the surface of the workbench. He had enough room to park a car, which showed how wrong the space was.

Real garages were an oily, messy disaster. She waited until the door closed then went to the rear of his car to pop the trunk. Time for him to wake up.

First, she heaved him out of the vehicle and hefted him to the only door in the space. She assumed it led inside. She leaned him against the doorjamb. "Wakey, wakey, my hot geek."

The man remained slumped, and she was the only thing between him and the gravity that wanted to mess up his pretty face.

She snapped her fingers.

Nothing.

Gave him a little shake.

His breathing remained steady, and his head still lolled.

If this were a fairy tale, she'd have already kissed him, maybe more. But Arik had a stern talking with them just last month about boundaries and stuff. Apparently, kissing random men fell under sexual harassment. But the biggest uproar occurred when he announced there would be no more ass slapping or butt pinches in public.

More than one lioness grumbled and complained, asking why they should have to suffer. As Jenny had said on more than one occasion, a man in tight jeans needed to know how much he was appreciated. Whistling was for wolves. Snorting was for pigs. Lionesses had perfected the art of ass pinching and slaps.

Alas, the king had spoken. Meaning, she had to be nice to the human or risk Arik's wrath.

She jiggled Theo and blew in his face. It proved to be enough to get him grimacing and stirring. His lashes fluttered open, and without his glasses, she noticed how thick they were.

"What's happening?" he asked, blinking at her. "Where are we?"

"Inside your garage, silly. Don't you remember me driving us home?"

His expression steadied. "No, I don't. Last thing I remember..." He frowned. "Why do I recollect gunmen storming the restaurant?"

"Ah, yes the evening's entertainment. You couldn't contain yourself and fell over."

"I did not. Someone hit me," he grumbled, touching the back of his head. "What the hell happened?"

"Gang fight and you didn't stay under the table like I told you to."

"Feels like I got clobbered by a train."

"Sweet talker." She almost blushed at his compliment.

"You said the men with guns were a gang."

"Did I?"

"Yes, and you knew them. One of them, at least. A guy named Percy, he came over to talk to you."

How to admit an interspecies rivalry? She couldn't, so she did the next best thing and lied her face off. "Fine, I guess I can't hide it. Percy is my ex-boyfriend."

"Does your ex-boyfriend show up often with friends toting guns?"

"What guns?" she asked in her most innocent voice.

He frowned. "I saw—"

"Don't you mean you thought you saw? Silly Theo. People don't take guns to restaurants, unless we're talking about the muscly kind." She squeezed his bicep.

He looked even more confused, and she felt the slightest bit of chagrin but not enough to tell him the truth. If Arik thought for one moment Theo might pose a threat to their secret...

Best not think about it.

Theo pushed away from the doorjamb, looking steadier by the moment. He patted his pockets, and she held up his keys, jangling them.

"Looking for these?"

His lips pressed into a tight line. He snatched the

keys and slotted them in the lock. With a twist and a click, the door opened.

For a moment, she expected him to say good night. But her geek was constantly surprising her.

"Want to come in?"

"Why yes, I would." She patted his cheek as she went by. "I thought you'd never ask."

CHAPTER FIVE

Theodore didn't know what had possessed him. The plan he'd devised from the moment he woke with a throbbing head was get inside, grab some acetaminophen, and sleep off the ache. Instead he'd opened his mouth and invited her inside. A stranger. Someone he'd been tasked with investigating. A known fraud and liar.

Worse?

She'd accepted—and immediately got the wrong impression.

A radiant smile on her face, Melly looped her arm in his and began blabbering. "Well, look at you, Mr. I'm-So-Stiff-You-Could-Use-Me-to-Push-a-Broom. Inviting me to check out your place after only the first date."

"That wasn't a date," he grumbled. Disaster came to mind.

"It had me, you, and food. That's a date, Poindexter."

"I am simply inviting you in until we can figure out how to get you home safely." Because he was in no condition to drive, which made him doubt her story of how they'd gotten here.

"You said 'we.'" She hugged him closer. "I knew you cared. Does this make us a couple?"

A couple, with this hot mess of crazy? Panic fluttered in his chest. "It most certainly does not. It was business."

"Fate."

"We met this afternoon."

"And already it seems like it's been longer. We were meant to be."

He skewed a stare at her and caught her snickering.

"Oh, the look on your face." She outright laughed. "Please. As if. You and I might bump body parts a few times for fun, but you are much too uptight for me to consider as a boyfriend."

True, and yet he was slightly offended. Perhaps he should rescind his offer for her to come in.

Too late.

Kicking off her shoes, she entered his space barefoot, and stared. Probably in awe at the crisp and clean perfection he'd achieved, unlike the hoarding conditions of her own place.

She whirled, her mouth agape to exclaim, "Oh my

God, this place is so boring. Did you get a discount for not using any color?"

He stiffened. "It's known as modern classic."

"It's dull. I mean it's gray everything."

"The walls and ceiling are white," he noted.

"With gray sepia prints on the wall."

"Some would say it's elegant."

"I'm sure the guy who sold you on this theme is snickering all the way to the bank. You need a makeover," she muttered, strutting farther into his compact bachelor apartment that comprised most of the first floor of the duplex. Condensed kitchen with a bar and stools to eat at, living room, and, off of it, a small study, which he kept locked, his bedroom, and bathroom.

She, of course, aimed for his private space.

He barely managed to interject himself. "I think it best if we stay in the main living area."

"Oooh, kinky. Are we doing it on the couch? The counter?"

"How about you believe me when I say no sex?"

She looked genuinely confused. "I don't get it. What's the point of inviting me in?"

He wasn't quite sure yet.

She wandered farther into his place, her very presence giving it a lively color overload.

"Have a seat. I'll mix us a drink." He pointed to the couch but couldn't help picture what she'd offered just a moment ago. Sex on the couch. It proved much too easy to imagine him sitting, her astride his lap. He stalked into the kitchen to hide any evidence of arousal. "What would you like?"

"Well, I was hoping for a hot geek injection, but I guess I'll settle for a beer."

"Er."

"Let me guess, you don't have beer." She stared at the ceiling and muttered, "Why me? What do you have?"

"Scotch. Whiskey. A bit of vodka."

"But no mix I'll bet."

"I have orange juice."

"Now you're talking."

Actually, his plan was to get her to talk. He'd yet to truly get a grasp on her—or those damning receipts. But what he'd learned thus far proved interesting, even as it made no sense.

He handed her a glass, which she downed and handed back. "Make the next one stronger."

He tripled the booze. She still downed it like water. Which was fine. He felt no guilt about getting her a little drunk. He wanted answers.

"So when are you going to tell me what really happened at the restaurant?"

"Whatever do you mean?" She batted her lashes so hard they almost took flight.

"I know those guys came in with guns and started shooting." He'd heard the popping.

"Fine. You got me." She sighed dramatically. "They were shooting, but it wasn't bullets."

"Then what?"

"Paint. A prank by a neighboring restaurant."

"Seems like a pretty intense prank. What if someone called the cops? They could have been shot."

"Good point. I'll be sure to tell Percy. Now, if we're done with that, let's talk about you."

He'd perched on the far end of the couch, and yet somehow, she'd ended up beside him. "Let's not."

He sidled away, but she remained close.

"Now, Theo, don't be shy."

"This isn't appropriate."

"It stopped being appropriate when you said yes to dinner."

"Because you promised to—"

She cut him off. "Oh, please. We both know you came to that restaurant because you like me. You think I'm pretty."

More than pretty but that wasn't the point. "Where are you getting your ammunition?"

"Oh, not that again." She sighed and flopped sideways on his couch. "Nice fabric." She then proceeded to toss the cushions onto the floor.

"What are you doing?" he exploded.

"Making myself comfortable. I like to sprawl." Which she proceeded to display, arms and legs akimbo.

A part of him wanted to join her. "I think it's time you left." Before things got out of hand.

"But I don't have a way home. Remember? I hitched a ride in your car."

"I'll call you a cab."

"You'd put me in a car with a stranger?" she huffed.

"Fine, then I'll drive you home."

"You really shouldn't be driving with that head injury," she stated, rolling on his cushions in a way that was both sinuous and suggestive.

"Surely there's someone you can call?" was his faint reply.

"Everyone's either in bed or partying. You're stuck with me, Poindexter."

"It's Theodore."

"Oooh look at you getting all tough with me. Any more orders you'd like to give?" She raised herself on her hands and knees, her smirk quite naughty.

"I think I need to go to bed."

Which once more showed her lack of sense of space. He went to his room and had turned around to bring her blankets and a pillow, only to discover she'd somehow moved from the couch cushions to his bed. Sprawled again.

"Um." At a loss for words, he looked down at the linen in his arms. The couch wasn't anywhere long enough to accommodate him. Yet the alternative...

He never managed to make it out of the room.

The woman, who had some kind of stealthy gene for sure, planted herself in front of him. "Where are you going? The bed is big enough for two."

A king size it was, and yet he knew it wouldn't be large enough. Like an idiot, who'd been getting dumber and dumber since meeting her earlier that day, he let her lead him to it. But he turned his back when she stripped.

Her soft chuckle caressed him. "I kept the bra and panties on, so you can relax. And I'm under the covers, so your delicate sensibilities won't be offended."

She did her best to goad, and it worked. He, the man of impeccable cool in any situation, was frazzled because of a half-naked woman.

It made his movements brisker than warranted as he stripped his jacket and shirt. His slacks, too. His boxers provided more cover than most bathing suits, but he still felt exposed. Stared at. Yet a short glance over his shoulder showed her lying on her side away from him.

In his bed. How had this happened?

One last time he thought of going out to the living room, but darn it, this was his bed. His home.

His job.

If they ever found out...he wouldn't be fired. More likely he'd get high-fives. He had a nickname around the office: the Ice Man. Apparently, it took the right kind of woman to make him melt.

"Are you coming to bed or not?"

"This is wrong," he muttered.

"Then leave." She rolled to face him, clad only in bra and panties, head propped on her hand.

She looked perfect there. And she was right. They'd met earlier that day, and yet it seemed much longer.

"I am not leaving my apartment."

"Neither am I, which means we're at an impasse, my sweet geek."

"This won't stop me from arresting you for tax fraud."

"I like a man with morals. They're more fun to corrupt." She winked.

She showed not the least bit of restraint. It usually would have roused his righteous nature, but instead, he got into the bed. It would take more than her allure to make him succumb.

To his surprise, she didn't try to touch him, but she did still talk. "Do you arrest people often for tax stuff?"

"Often enough." The scent of her wrapped around him, teasing him with a tickle in the nose. Just a little one. He hoped he didn't sneeze again. He still had no idea what came over him in the restaurant. It was emasculating to the extreme.

"Theodore Loomer, IRS agent extraordinaire. So does arresting people sometimes mean you have cuffs?" She sounded so hopeful.

"Yeah."

"Really?" She bounced to her knees, and his gaze drifted to the valley between her breasts. "Can I see them?"

"You'll see them soon enough if you don't provide proper receipts and documentation," he warned.

"You are no fun."

"I'm okay with it." He truly was. Yet for a moment, as she sighed and turned on her side away from him, he wished he was a different kind of man. The kind to drag her into his arms and kiss her.

He did nothing, and soon she softly snored. Whereas he lay awake, no further ahead in his task than before. Perhaps sleeping together, with him respecting her, would get her to trust him and explain the weaponry. No one needed that much firepower. What of the strange arrangement she had with the Pride Group? No company was that generous. Was it all linked to the incident at the restaurant? Perhaps he should tell Maverick to look more closely at that location, too. Gang war indeed.

Something else was afoot. He could sense it. The lies, the subterfuge. He just needed to dig a little deeper.

The night passed in spurts of sleep, short jolts of fifteen minutes here and there. During it all, she didn't move. Didn't sprawl or touch him in any way, and yet he was so aware of her.

Too aware. When dawn hit, he eased out of the bed and went into his bathroom. He looked haggard. Unshaven, his eyes a bit bloodshot. He scrubbed a hand over his jaw. First thing, he turned on the shower, stripped his boxers, and stepped under the hot spray. He put his face into it, letting the heat seep into his pores, his muscles, his soul.

He tried to relax, and yet he couldn't help thinking of the woman in his bed. Would she wake up and leave, maybe embarrassed at her forward actions surely caused by the drink?

Would she continue to vex him or...? The shower curtain rustled, and he whirled.

"What are you doing?" he managed to exclaim, shocked to discover she'd joined him.

"I woke up all alone, so I came to find you. Share the water." She shoved past him, her body naked and slick.

A smart man would have left at that point. But he had no blood left in his brain to think.

He stood there as she turned her face into the spray and opened her mouth to let it run into it and spill over. He was only human and couldn't keep his gaze from devouring the sight of her wet body, the frame of her tight and yet flaring at the hips. Her breasts small, the nipples tiny rosebuds. The hair between her legs damp and dark with moisture.

She grabbed the soap and lathered her hands before touching him.

His voice emerged rough. "I can wash myself."

"It's more fun if I do it."

On that count she was right, but this was wrong. He grabbed her wrists and held her hands away from him. "You have to stop this. I'm not going to clear you just because you have sex with me."

"Sex? Who says we're having sex? I'm hungry in the morning, and you have just what I need," she said with a wink before she dropped to her knees.

Surely, she wouldn't.

She grabbed hold of him. "Try and relax."

An impossible task given her hands on his cock were anything but.

Her hot breath fluttered over the flesh of his shaft as she blew on the wet length of it. And it was lengthy. He couldn't hide his arousal. Didn't actually want to. Seduction wasn't part of his plan, and yet he did nothing to stop it.

She gripped him in an eager hand, stroking his flesh. A cry escaped him when she decided to stop teasing with hot breaths and take him into her mouth. She gave him a good hard suck. Then another. She bobbed her head on his cock, and he could only lean his head back and enjoy.

It was possible he enjoyed it more than he should have given it was so very taboo. Theo wasn't usually the type to be distracted on the job, but that was only because he'd never met Melly.

She ate him with gusto, sucking and slurping at him until he thought he would go mad. When she let his shaft loose with a wet pop, he couldn't help a sound of disappointment.

He reached for her and dragged her upright, mashing his mouth to hers, giving in to the temptation of tasting her lips.

She protested. "I wasn't done with you."

Words to increase the ache in his cock and the tightness of his balls. "Maybe it's your turn." Where did he find those husky words? He wasn't one to usually talk during the act.

"Oh no you don't, my sexy nerd. I've been

dreaming of sucking that cock of yours. which means you don't get a turn on me until I'm done." With that warning and promise, she dropped back onto her haunches and grabbed him. Firmly.

Her other hand cradled his balls. His hips jerked, and he uttered a low groan as she once more sheathed him with her mouth. Hers lip slid down the length of his shaft, right to the root.

He didn't know how she did it, but it felt better than good. It was amazing. And arousing. Especially when she began to bob and suck on him, her cheeks hollowing every time she pulled. He would know. He watched.

They fell into a cadence, her head held in place by his hands as his hips bucked to fill her mouth.

The pressure of his orgasm had him panting. He was going to come. In her mouth. A new thing for him. What if she didn't want it? What if—

"You're thinking too much again," she advised, the words rumbling around his flesh.

"It's my turn," he managed to say when all he really wanted to do was let go.

"I'm not done." She worked his cock, swirling her tongue around the swollen head. Sucked it. Tasted it. Even nibbled on it. She played with him, and he couldn't help but dig his fingers into her scalp, thrusting his cock at her.

And when she squeezed and kneaded his balls?

He came.

In her mouth.

CHAPTER SIX

Mmm. She did so like cream, and his was tastier than most.

Melly would have liked to remain in the shower for part two, where he used that tongue of his for something other than arguing; however, she'd checked her phone before joining her sexy geek, and if she didn't get her butt home, Arik was going to send the Biatches after her. Given they would just barge in and ogle her Theo, best she get moving.

She let go of his cock, and he slumped against the wall. Now there was a sight to make a woman grin. She stood and would have stepped out of the shower, only she found herself pushed against the tile, her geek not as far-gone as she thought. His expression smoldered.

"Where do you think you're going?"

"I have a meeting."

"It can wait." He growled the words. Not a shifter

growl but that of a man who desired her. "I'm not done with you."

He thrust his hand between her thighs, and she mewled as he stroked her. He'd had his pleasure, and yet he wanted to give her some in return.

Melly wasn't about to say no, not when he knelt between her legs and parted them. He wasted no time finding her core, his tongue parting her lips for a taste. Her leg went over his shoulder at his urging, opening her up to him, and he took advantage.

She'd never been so well eaten in her life. He knew just how to play with her clitoris, teasing it with his lips, rubbing his tongue so hard and fast she was panting in no time, tearing at his scalp.

He grunted against her, showing a pure enjoyment that would have made her come. She wanted to come, but he stopped.

She made a pathetic mewling sound.

"Tell me where you bought the ammo," he asked against her throbbing flesh.

Seriously? Now he wanted to talk business? She stiffened.

He thrust a finger into her, and she gasped.

"Tell me and I'll finish you off."

Sex for secrets? It was very un-nerd like and surprisingly hot. "I can masturbate if you don't."

"You could." He blew on then spent a moment rubbing her clit until she panted. He continued as if he'd not just driven her crazy. "Or I could offer you a deal. Immunity for info."

"Immunity for me and my friends, plus you make me come."

He pressed his thumb against her clit. "You're asking a lot."

"I'd be risking even more telling you." She ground herself against his hand.

"Deal. Start talking."

"I get the ammo in the tunnels."

"What tunnels?" He stretched her with a second finger.

"Under the city. But the location moves around." She gyrated her hips.

"Can you take me?"

"No."

"Wrong answer." He withdrew his fingers.

"Fine. Yes. I'll take you." The fingers returned, along with his tongue and a whispered, "When?"

"Next week."

He stopped.

"Tonight?" she squeaked, her pleasure on the edge.

"Promise?"

"Yes!" she said on a breathy high note as he finished her.

His tongue swept her clit, and his fingers thrust into her until her blessed orgasm hit. A shuddering thing that left her weak and satisfied, even more than the fresh cream she'd stolen from the condo's kitchens last week.

She'd just been outmaneuvered by the human, and he knew it, too. Smug bastard. He stood, looking very pleased with himself. With good reason. He'd pleasured her well.

She wanted to purr. Scratch. Ride him until they both came again.

But there was a pounding heard even from the shower.

"Who is that?" He turned his head, his expression stern. For a moment Theo looked almost dangerous.

For a human.

She patted his cheek. "My ride. Thanks for the morning nookie."

He grabbed at her as she stepped out of the shower. "You can't leave yet."

"I can and I am." She slipped free and left with the only towel in the bathroom.

As he dove into the cupboard for another, she shut the bathroom door and wedged a chair under the handle. That would hold him for a minute while she dressed.

He banged on the door, most unhappy with her. Only when she'd finished getting her clothes on did she remove the barrier and skip to the front door.

He emerged from the bedroom wearing only a towel around his hips, a sight that tempted her to stay. She might have totally climbed his damp body, only she heard Joan hollering.

"Biatch, get your ass out here before we drag you out. We have business to attend to."

Melly blew him a kiss and said, "Later, Theo."

Rather than reply, he turned to head back into his room, the towel dropping to show his firm ass.

She almost told Joan to leave without her. But duty to the Pride called.

She detoured by her place for a change of gear. No need for the boss to smell what she'd been doing. He still guessed.

As she walked into Arik's office, he roared, "You slept with the guy from the IRS."

"He had a bed big enough for two. But don't worry, nothing happened in it."

"You're lying," Arik seethed.

"Not exactly. We screwed around in the shower, not his bed. Didn't have time given you sent Joan to drag me out."

"When Reba informed me this morning where you ended up, you're damned straight I had you extracted."

"Relax, he knows nothing."

"He was there when the bears invaded. He had to have seen something."

"I broke his glasses and stuffed him under a table. I promise he didn't see a thing."

Arik scrubbed at his face. "I hope you're right, but even if you are, what the hell were you thinking? A human in the back side of the restaurant?"

She was thinking she wanted to show off, which made no sense. It wasn't as if Theo was her prize.

"You did it with Kira."

"Because Kira was my mate. Are you trying to tell me something?" The king arched a brow.

She couldn't help but gasp a horrified, "No!"

Never. Not with Theo. A human. A geek who actually didn't lay a hand on her while they were in bed. What man didn't try to at least fake a snuggle?

"So if you're not about to bite the man and claim him as yours, why the fuck are you bringing him places he shouldn't be?"

The king knew how to raise his voice without actually getting louder. She might have shriveled a little. But a lioness never fully cowered. She twisted the situation.

"He offered me a deal."

"What kind of deal?" Arik asked, drumming his fingers on his desk.

"The kind that sees them dropping the tax fraud investigation."

"Which is a whole other issue. What the hell were you thinking? We have accountants you can use. Safeguards to avoid attention."

"The program I devised needs tweaking."

"Too late now, isn't it?"

"I'll take care of it," she muttered.

"In return for what? Because he's obviously not doing it for free."

"Some things are priceless." She tossed her hair.

"Your confidence in your skills is admirable, but I am fairly certain he wanted more than that."

Melly scowled. "I promised I'd take him to my ammo supplier."

"You what!" The roar shook the windows.

She cringed. "I know, I messed up."

"Actually, this might work in our favor. If you bring him down into those tunnels, he likely won't emerge alive."

Her turn to gape at the king. "You want him to die."

"It's not as if you are leaving me much choice. And don't be mad at me. We wouldn't be in this situation if it weren't for your creative accounting."

She hung her head. "I learned my lesson."

"I doubt you have yet, but you will. Take the man to the tunnels and let nature sort itself."

"What if he comes out alive?"

Arik pinned her with a gaze that only a king could imbue with such force. "Are you or are you not a Pride huntress?"

"I am."

"Then I trust you'll make sure that doesn't happen."

Kill the man who'd played her so well she'd spilled secrets? She wondered if there was time for one more round before she led him to his doom.

CHAPTER SEVEN

M elly left after he made her come. No kiss. No nothing. Just a vague promise extracted in the shower that she would take him to the person selling ammo, who might be completely legit. He doubted it, though.

He couldn't say why he had a gut feeling he should follow up on that lead. It wasn't part of his mandate, but Theodore knew Maverick would be interested in it. Even if he wasn't, he had friends in ATF who would be.

However, he had no idea if she'd actually follow through. She could just as easily say no again as yes. Would she make him resort to teasing her sexually to get another promise?

He could almost only hope.

Dammit. What had he done? Sleeping with her had complicated his job rather than easing it.

Heading into the office, he wore a scowl, not that

anyone noticed. He didn't come by his nickname Ice Man by being warm and friendly.

It didn't help that Maverick soon called him into his office.

"Well, where are we on the Pride investigation?" Maverick focused on him.

"Still investigating. I've met with one of the subjects but not gotten far." In the case at least. He'd gone to third base in other things.

"How much are they denying?"

"Nothing yet. The one I've interviewed admits to claiming illegal ammo on her taxes."

"And Pride Industries is involved."

"Not exactly. The way she spoke her supplier isn't part of that group. I'll know more after I meet with them tonight."

"A meeting. Most excellent." Maverick appeared pleased, which was why Theodore laid out the part he wouldn't like next.

"I might have promised Melly, I mean Ms. Goldeneyes, immunity in exchange for the information on her ammo dealer."

"What?" Maverick exploded.

Now probably wasn't the time to admit he'd also included her friends and family. "I needed her to trust me."

"You shouldn't have made that promise. I can't guarantee anything until I know more about the situation."

A hint of guilt flooded Theo. "What if she gives me more intel?"

"It better be more than just an arms supplier."

"I'll see what I can find."

Leaving the office, he had just enough time to drive across town for his next arranged meeting at the Pride condominium complex. Melly had threatened to see him later. She'd not said what time or where. If it happened at all.

In the meantime, perhaps someone else would spill something that would make Maverick happy. Or, at the very least, stop making Theo contemplate the merits of going postal. Or in that case, would it be going taxing?

He pulled up to the gate, and this time was buzzed right in. He parked out front in one of three spots marked for visitors. When he walked in, someone in the lounge area shouted, "It's the IRS dude. Hide your assets, ladies."

Which involved the buttoning of cleavage and engendered much giggling.

He was not amused. He turned on his heel to give them all a proper glare. He was wearing his spare glasses. He had several, given accidents happened, especially with how often he went into sneezing fits. Funny how he wasn't as bothered by his allergies today upon entering.

"Not divulging your earnings for assessment is a federal crime," he reminded them since he had their attention.

"So is putting sticks up asses, but here we are," muttered someone else.

Said stick only made his back straighter. "I'm here on business."

"I'll bet you are," was a feminine snicker. "But Melly's not here. She's doing something for Arik."

Arik? A spurt of jealousy quickly died as he recalled that was the name of her employer. Was she doing some of the security work she'd claimed the day before?

Didn't matter. "I'm not here to see Ms. Gold-eneyes. If you'll excuse me, ladies." He turned away and heard laughter.

"He called us ladies."

"Because he recognizes class."

"You wouldn't know class if your thong hit you with it."

"Say that to my face, biatch.

Despite the inciting words, he doubted it would come to a fight. A place this upscale wouldn't cater to those with the baser instinct to brawl.

Then again...

As the elevator doors closed, he could have sworn he saw a body flying over a couch. Surely a trick of the light.

This time he went to the sixth floor, found the right door, and knocked.

When the portal opened, a blonde woman, almost the same height as him, eyed him up and down. "Well, aren't you pretty."

Flustered, he remembered his job. "Mrs. Vander-coop, I'm Theodore Loomer with the IRS. We have an appointment to discuss your taxes."

Her eyes widened. "Shoot, is that today? Give me a second."

The door slammed shut, leaving him outside in the hall. He frowned. Especially since he could hear all kinds of noise, banging and thumping. His nose twitched. He took another allergy med, third one this morning. He wasn't planning on sneezing anytime soon.

He knocked. "Mrs. Vandercoop, I'm not worried about the tidiness of your home. I'm here to discuss your taxes."

It took more banging inside before the door opened on a now flushed and much more disheveled woman. She smiled. "Just doing a little putting away. I don't often get male company. Won't you come in?"

Entering, he noticed the apartment was much cleaner than Melly's. The floors were clear of debris and dishes. The counters shone. The furniture was actually usable. What was odd was the distinct lack of anything on the walls, made stranger by the hooks on them, as if something used to hang in brackets but had been removed.

She caught him looking. "I, er, um, broke up with my boyfriend. You know how it is, out with the old." She grinned widely. Not reassuringly.

"Shall we get to business?" He gestured to the table. "May I?"

"Go right ahead. I've got nothing to hide."

"That would be a change," he muttered as he put his briefcase down and opened it. He pulled forth a new file. It held even less information than the one on Melly.

Either these women truly stayed out of the public eye or someone did a good job of scrubbing them. Which was just paranoid. Most petty criminals tended to be brazen. It was how they got caught.

He'd just managed to flip open the file when the perfume hit him. A glance to his left almost had him falling off the chair. Mrs. Vandercoop had chosen to perch close to him. Very close.

"You smell good," she said. "What cologne are you wearing?"

"Soap."

"No, it's more than that." She leaned in and inhaled. "Oh, look at you. So many interesting things going on."

He feared knowing what that meant. "Do you have the receipts for your last tax return so we can go through them?"

"A man of business. I like it. Of course, I have my receipts. They're in the bedroom. Give me just a second."

She left, and he glanced around the apartment with its slick décor. Similar in style to his, if more colorful. He wondered what used to hang on the walls. The sets of hooks reminded him of those used to hang swords. But who would need so many? And why hide them?

"Oh, Mr. IRS man, can you come here for a minute?" her voice called from the bedroom.

"I don't think that's a good idea." As a matter of fact, he knew for sure it was a bad one.

"But I need your help. The box with the paper-work is on a high shelf."

And how was he supposed to help with that given she was just as tall as he was? "Don't you have a stool or a chair to stand on?"

"I do, yet what if I fall off? I just need someone to steady me."

It sounded reasonable enough.

Theodore entered a room covered in rose gold and tassels. So many tassels. They hung from the chande-lier in glittering crystals. From the corners of the pillows in thick strands. Even the edges of the comforter and carpet had tassels.

"Where are you?" he asked.

"In the closet."

Walking in, Theodore found more tassels hanging from Mrs. Vandercoop's nipples. He averted his gaze.

"Ma'am, you appear to have misplaced your shirt."

"Have you ever seen the Tassel Dance up close?" she asked. Jerking her torso, she slapped him with the stringy fabric.

"Your actions are most unsuitable."

"Is that your way of calling me old?"

"Hardly. You seem to forget I am not here to act as your entertainment but to do my job."

"Isn't your job to examine me? Here I am. Ready for inspection."

"I'm leaving." He turned on his heel and would have left the closet had he not come face to face with a scowl. "Melly?" He couldn't help the surprise in the word.

"Hello, Theo. Imagine finding you here. Aunt Marissa." The name emerged flat and hard.

"Did you need something, dear niece? As you can see, I'm busy."

"I'll just bet you are," Melly muttered. "Would you excuse us a moment, Theo? I need to speak to my aunt."

"We have a meeting."

"In her closet?" Melly asked. "And after what you and I did? That's tacky."

He opened and shut his mouth before exclaiming, "Nothing happened."

"Only because I arrived."

"Now, Melly..." the older woman said.

"Not yet, Auntie. Now, Theee-o-o, if you please." She drew out his name.

He wasn't about to argue with the look in her eyes. There was something a little wild and untamed in that angry gaze. Jealous, too.

He'd never had a woman jealous over him before. The novelty intrigued. He sat back at the table with the open file as the door to the bedroom closed. What was happening inside? He imagined Mrs. Vandercoop was about to get a tongue lashing from her niece. A well-deserved one.

His theory proved true, or so he surmised, as he heard voices, one of them raised and fast-talking then a lower, calmer murmur that he just knew belonged to Melly. The subdued nature of it turned into banging. Something kept thumping the wall, enough times he almost went to see. When the door eventually opened, Melly emerged looking smug, and Mrs. Vandercoop had found her clothes and a fat lip.

She also had a check that she thrust at him.

"My apologies for trying to defraud the government. Take this and go."

The number of zeroes would more than pay for any fine. Dammit. But he'd never even gotten a chance to see any of her paperwork. "It's not that simple."

Mrs. Vandercoop eyed Melly, whose arms were crossed over her chest. Her expression held a slightly amused twist.

"It will have to be that simple, as I've got an appointment I have to make. If I owe more, then send me a bill and I'll mail another check."

Melly jumped in. "You heard my aunt. You're done here."

"She never showed me her papers."

"Because there's no need since she's not claiming them anymore. Time—as little Cecilia says—to vamoose."

"But—"

In moments, Theodore found himself in the hall, bewildered at how things had transpired. Relieved at the rescue, but mostly confused. "How did you know I was with your aunt?"

"Word travels in the complex," was Melly's grumbled complaint. "My phone lit up more than on my birthday with people letting me know my geek was paying Auntie a visit."

"I never encouraged her." It seemed important he let her know.

"Never figured you did. Since my uncle ran off with a woman from back east, she's indulged in lusty proclivities."

"It was kind of scary," he admitted as she led him down the hall to the stairs. Six floors down.

"You should be terrified. Those things can take out an eye. Try explaining that to the cops when they show up claiming she assaulted that guy."

He paused in the stairs. "You're kidding, right?"

The greenish golden gaze she turned his way could have hidden anything. Truth, dare, amusement. "Stay away from my aunt."

Funny how it sounded like a threat meant for him.

She opened the door on the fifth floor, getting ready to leave.

He blurted out the first thing that came to mind. "What time are we meeting your arms dealer?"

She let the door close and stalked close to him, hissing. "Shh, you idiot. Don't let anyone hear you."

"There's no one here."

"That you can see. But sound travels. We don't want them being tipped off."

"What's wrong with you bringing a potential new client?"

She stared at him in utter amazement, and yet he'd done nothing. "You really have no idea how it works. So protected." She patted his cheek. "Come on. Let's go to my apartment."

"Don't you mean the cesspool of doom?"

He'd not meant to say it aloud and yet he had, and she laughed, a wondrous bubbly sound that warmed.

"You're lucky. Today was cleaning day."

Apparently, it was also one for miracles. He walked into a vastly different space with gleaming floors and counters, not a speck of dirt to be seen, and all the cushions on the couch.

"It's like walking into an alternate universe," he muttered, to which she giggled.

"Way to show off your nerd."

"I am anything but," he argued. A nerd wouldn't have such lusty thoughts about a case file. In the past he'd never struggled to separate job from fantasy. This time, he wanted to say to hell with the job.

"You are so a nerd. And I can prove it," Melly exclaimed. "Your clothes are on hangers sorted by color."

No point in asking how she knew. She'd obviously snooped in his closet.

"That's only partly correct. I also group them by season."

"That's nuts."

"I don't see how. When you think of the different needs of each season, it just makes sense."

"I'll bet the stuff in your drawers is folded."

"How else would you put it away?" He couldn't help genuine bafflement. Why bother even opening a drawer to stow clothing if it wasn't rolled a la Marie Kondo? His uncluttered efficiency had increased tenfold after reading her book.

"If I went into your kitchen right now, I'll bet you the cans are all label facing forward and alphabetized."

"They are not."

At her pointed stare, he shrugged. "Label forward, but I group them by type. Vegetable, soup, fruit."

"Aha! I knew it!"

"That doesn't make me a nerd." He knew how the world perceived so-called geeks. He couldn't have said why it was important to him that she not see him as weak.

"Have you watched *Star Wars* more than three times?" She fired the question at him.

"Only the originals," he hotly defended.

"Whereas I have watched *Spaceballs* about a hundred, *Sharknado* at least a dozen, and I cry my eyes out every single time I watch *The Lion King*."

He didn't admit his secret love for *Spaceballs*, especially when they combed the desert. It always drew a chuckle. "I like comedies and animated classics."

"Tell me a fart joke."

He blinked. "Excuse me?"

"You can't, can you? Because a) you don't know one and b) you wouldn't repeat it even if you did."

She had him pegged all wrong. She seemed to think because he followed the rules, he was staid and boring with no sense of humor, which was why he quite enjoyed saying, "What happens if you fart in church?" Before she could reply, he answered. "You have to sit in your own pew. Why shouldn't you ever fart on an elevator? Because it's wrong on every single level." He finished with, "If farting at the speed of sound, would you hear it or smell it first?"

She gaped at him and then offered him the biggest, brightest smile. "Oh, my dear Theo. There might be hope for you yet."

"Because I can tell an off-color joke?"

"Because you have a sense of humor, not to mention a talented tongue." She pinched his chin. "A pity we don't have time for a repeat."

Why didn't they have time? "You brokered a deal for yourself and the others in your building that owed, so why did you make your aunt pay?"

"Because she irritated me. She knew better than to play with my toy." She patted his cheek and sashayed off.

The cuteness didn't belay his irritation. "I am not your toy."

She cast him a sloe-eyed glance over her shoulder. "Does that mean no more playing with you?"

"No. Yes. Dammit, Melly!"

"There's the passion. I knew you had it in you."

"That's not passion; it's annoyance. You're intentionally goading me."

"Because you make it so easy."

"Have you forgotten your fate and that of your family is in my hands?"

"How could I?" She batted her lashes in a manner that was anything but deprecating. "I am ever so grateful for what you're doing. I mean, what girl doesn't want to have the threat of jail time used as blackmail so you can get what you want?"

The astuteness of the accusation roused guilt and a rare heat in his cheeks. "It's not blackmail. Merely an alternative to your situation."

Her throaty chuckle touched him and brought a shiver. "You can call it what you like, Theo. It's extortion, pure and simple. But lucky for you, I don't mind. You want to meet my ammo supplier, then so be it. Just don't blame me if things go sideways." A sad cast pulled down the corners of her lips.

"You won't be implicated. My office will merely ensure they are conducting their business legally and if not notify the appropriate channels."

Melly snorted. "They're selling ammo that's banned for civilian use in the USA. Of course, they're not legal. But that's between you, whatever division you narc for, and them. Although I will say don't come crying when they break your kneecaps."

"I'll be fine."

"You're so cute when you're wrong." She shook her

head, and he had to wonder if he'd imagined that moment in the shower.

The wanton woman. The passion...

"What time are we going?"

"Soon. But I have to change first." She began to strip, showing just how her place got wrecked each week.

The shirt hit the floor, and unthinking, he bent to grab it, following in her wake. Her pants were around her ankles as he walked into the bedroom. She kicked them across the floor as she headed for the closet. Her thong formed a heart at the top of her ass.

He leaned to get the clothes on the floor, and she turned, presenting him with the red heart fabric barely covering her mound.

"Mmm. Theo. Naughty boy. If only we had time, but Marney keeps very strict office hours. If we're going to make this work, we have to make it quick."

He might have stupidly asked what work, only, as he straightened, she pushed him until his back hit a wall. Her mouth meshed with his, the kiss hot and consuming. The lust rose quick within.

Her hands unbuckled his pants and freed him, her grasp firm, his gasp loud. She angled his cock toward her pussy, but she was too short for it to work, so she climbed him. Her arms around his neck, she wrapped her legs around his hips and held on. A good thing the wall held him because, without any kind of real fore-play, she impaled herself on him.

He shouted, and his hands automatically gripped

her ass, digging his fingers in. She didn't need much from him. She bounced, flexing and grinding, driving his dick deep inside, the channel of her sex squeezing him.

She came quickly, and he followed, shouting as he spurted hotly. Knowing he was acting out of character. He'd forgotten to even slip a condom from his pocket, and she'd never paused. Surely, she took birth control.

As for anything else…there were clinics for that. Not the sexiest thought, given she panted against him.

She sighed. "Oh, that hit the spot." Off she sprang, hitting the floor and tugging her panties back over her ass.

"We should sluice off," he said, knowing the scent of sex would cling to them both.

The grin she tossed had a mischievous glint to it. "I don't plan to, and take my advice; you'll want the scent of me on you, too. It will prevent any misunderstandings as to your position."

"I fail to see what you could possibly mean."

"Trust me. You don't want to meet Marney as a single man. You'll get eaten up."

"So you're going to have me pretend to be your boyfriend?"

At that, she laughed. "As if Marney would believe that. You're going as my boy toy. Lucky you, I have just the right outfit."

CHAPTER EIGHT

The look on his face?
        Priceless.

Especially when she found the leather-studded collar and asked if he wanted to wear it to complete his ensemble.

"I am not going as some sex slave," Theo hotly retorted.

He looked so adorable with his tie slightly askew. Color in his cheeks, his lips...Mmm, the things those lips could do.

"What about submissive? My love muffin? How about hot meat on a walking stick?"

He glared, and her amusement only grew. In the end, he refused her offers to dress him so that he would fit in. Not the smartest choice. He had no idea he was about to enter a world that would eat him up. Literally.

The guilt over what she planned bit her hard. Never mind her orders, she was walking him into a trap. He had no clue. It was bothersome enough she wanted to scream. Shake him a little and warn him to run far and fast. Not that it would matter. The pride hunters would find him.

Knowing he was doomed hadn't stopped her from having sex. She couldn't help herself. Being with him ignited her mind and body.

If only he were somebody else. A shapeshifter like her. Or someone that could handle the truth like Arik's mate, Kira. But Theo was so damned rigid. He'd probably turn them over to his government pals, and then bad stuff would really happen.

Such a shame he had to die.

However, she wouldn't make it easy. She would try and offer him some protection, and that started with the right outfit. She needed to convey a bad biatch on the loose vibe. A touch my man and I will rip off your arm and beat you with it kind of air.

To that end, she wore ripped jeans, tight in all the right places, lacings keeping the seams shut on each side. A quick release if she needed to change shapes. A black tank top that would tear easily. No undies. Because if she had to shift, she'd rather they not get caught in her tail. She still remembered the fiasco that year she dressed up as a certain superhero. When it came time to shift, she got stuck in her fancy outfit. Luna loved to send her that pic every year to remind her.

With any luck, there shouldn't be any need for her feline tonight. When Marney demanded she leave Theo with them, Melly would agree and walk away.

Rowr. Her feline side didn't like that idea one bit. Odd how she seemed to really like the human. She blamed it on boredom. Her other half hadn't been out for a run in a while. She sought entertainment anywhere.

Soon, my sweet kitty. The full moon approached. While she could control herself, it would be harder if she didn't soon blow off some lion steam.

Strutting out of her room, she found Theo sitting on a kitchen stool. He pivoted when he heard her. The appreciation in his gaze almost made her delay again. What if the last time truly was the last time?

Then she'd have obeyed her king.

"I need a drink and so do you."

"Alcohol is probably not a good idea right now."

She tossed him a smile over her shoulder. "It's always a good idea. Just one for courage."

"I'm fine." As if to defy him, his body reacted, and he sneezed.

She had something to fix that. She went to the cupboard and pulled out two shot glasses.

"You will have a shot with me. And you will like it. Understood?" She pulled out a bottle of cinnamon Fireball that made even her eyes water, but it would mask any taste.

She held out the small glass, and he hesitated before snatching it.

She tapped hers against his. "Bottoms up." She

tilted it and, the moment it hit her mouth, quickly swallowed. It burned, her mouth caught on cinnamon fire. She gasped, certain she'd see flames.

She blinked watering eyes to see Theo looking as calm as ever. A quick peek at his glass showed it empty.

"Damn, Poindexter."

"If we're done?"

"Oh, I'm not done with you yet, but that will have to wait until later."

With lips painted a shocking red, she kissed him, leaving a visible mark that he didn't know to wipe off. Her sweet geek had no idea how to handle someone like her. He'd never get the chance either if she didn't take care of him.

Surely there was a way to make Arik happy and keep Theo alive. She just had to think of it. She snared Theo by the hand and dragged him downstairs. "We'll take my bike."

"That deadly crotch rocket? I don't think so."

"Is that supposed to be a commentary on female drivers?"

"No, it's because I'm well aware of your driving record. Three fender benders and six tickets."

"The German autobahns don't have speed limits."

"Because they expect people to use common sense. I wouldn't recommend you move there."

Her mouth rounded as he managed a very good dig. "That was well done. But we're still taking my bike."

"I can drive."

She shook her head. "Your car screams federal employee. All boring and shit. That kind of vehicle isn't ever seen in the part of town we're going. Besides, we won't be riding for long. We'll be parking the bike and going mostly on foot." The underground tunnels weren't exactly conducive to automotive travel. Although hoverboards and Segways were popular. She really should get one, or both. She and the other lionesses could have races. She'd always wondered if the boards would hover more than a few inches off the ground, say off the edge of a building.

"I am not dressed to ride. I don't even have a helmet."

"Don't worry. I'll protect that sweet noggin of yours."

He didn't seem impressed when she borrowed the bright pink helmet belonging to Delaney.

"I am not wearing this," he flatly stated.

"Is your masculinity threatened?" she asked sweetly, dangling it by one strap.

"It says PMS Princess."

"More like rampaging diva. We were being polite when we got it for her birthday."

He crossed his arms and refused to touch it. "Find me something plain."

"Giving me orders? Who would have thought it?"

"Just because I like cerebral things doesn't mean I'm a pushover."

"I'll be damned. You gave me shit, and yet did it in

a sexy way. How can I resist?" She tweaked his nose. "Give me a second."

He accepted the simple blue helmet she found, and when he climbed behind her on the bike, she got a secret thrill at the feel of his arms around her. She'd never tell her friends. They'd mock her for sure.

Theo was a fun partner in bed. An entertaining person, but she had to remind herself he was human, meaning fragile. Given his nature, he might not fit in too easily with the rest of the pride. Especially given her role. The hunters couldn't afford weakness of any kind.

Pity. Because she really, really liked him.

Theo held on tight as she sped them through the city streets. With the waning day, the traffic lessened in some areas, increased in others, but not where they were going. The only vehicles there tended to have noisy mufflers, souped-up frames and blaring music. The buses ran every hour, only because they had to. Rumor had it the drivers earned hazard pay. Not that it was truly all that bad, so long as you paid your dues and stayed on the Hyena Clan's good side. Their matriarch ran a tight, laughter-filled crew.

The lions tended to avoid them, but given Marney was only accessible via Hyena territory, an exception had to be made.

The neon of the seedy motel's sign flashed—three of the letters were burnt out or intentionally broken so that it went from spelling Slick and Buttery Hotel to Lick Butt Ho. It sold beds by the hour in an environment that even she would think twice about staying too long in.

Delaney had gotten fleas from a date she had with a married guy at this hourly rental. Fleas which spread. Before they contained it, too many of them got itchy bites. But the embarrassing part was running out of the topical solution and having to wear those stupid white collars for a week while they fumigated the condos.

Theo let go of her and got off the bike, pulling the helmet off. He didn't look half as disheveled as he did when they were making out. It was a source of pride.

"This is where we're meeting your contact??" he asked, looking around. He set the helmet on the seat of the bike.

As if it would stay there. Already she felt the eyes watching them. Coveting her things. Her gaze slewed from her motorcycle to Theo.

My things. Time to make it clear who the bike and the man belonged to. With her back to Theo, Melly snarled at the shadows, letting the glow in her eyes shine, her teeth show. Letting them know what would happen if they messed with her. She'd eat them to prove a point and protect Theo. And who cared what Arik wanted?

Her gaze froze on Theo, and she frowned. The instinct to guard him seemed unusually strong. She didn't usually have heroic tendencies for those outside the pride. She also tended to avoid dragging most people along when she went to meet dangerous arms dealers.

Yet he'd left her no choice. The deal to get her and the other biatches out of trouble was too good to pass up. Not her problem if the feds went after Marney for taxes and other stuff. The dealer had been asking for it of late anyhow. Dealing in things other than arms.

Lab-produced drugs were bad. Why couldn't people just be happy and mellow smoking weed?

By the end of today, either Marney would be dealing with the IRS or Melly would be having a drink, toasting the geek she used to know.

Melly led him inside the motel, wishing she could have dressed him so he wouldn't stick out. Then again, maybe he'd be fine. This was a place where even the uptight in their nice suits came to indulge in their vices. They were easy to spot as they arrived, nervous and twitching.

Not Theo, though. He had a stiff yet prideful posture to him, and he took in entirely too much. What did he think of the walls with their stains and marks of violence from the years?

What of the person behind the reception counter with their rainbow-tinted hair, heavily done eye shadow, and pouty lips? They didn't even look at Theo and Melly as they passed by.

Melly opened a door marked utility. Metal stairs creaked as they went down, leading into a room filled with machinery, pipes, and wires. There was a surprising lack of debris and cobwebs. Probably because the metal hatch in the floor provided entrance to yet another level below.

"How far down are we going?" he asked, a hint of caution in his tone.

"Hard to say in feet, but it's deeper than this. There are tunnels under the city. Some of them current. Some of them old. All of them interconnected."

"And that's where this Marney person lives?"

"I don't know if they live there, but Marney definitely only does business in one of their lairs."

"Implying more than a few. How many are there?"

She shrugged. "I've seen two. Josee says she's seen three, and one of her meeting spots doesn't sound like any I've visited. So who knows really?"

"How do we know where Marney is then?"

"Because we'll have an escort of course. Surely you didn't think they'd just let us walk in." The moment she said it, they hit the last step and heard the click of guns.

She knew to raise her hands, but Theo looked around like he was at some meet-and-greet. "Hello, I'm here to make a purchase."

He couldn't have sounded more like a narc if he tried.

The girl with the pink and green ponytail nudged him with the tip of her gun. "What the fuck? Did you rat us out to the popo?" she accused.

Since lying would only get him killed, Melly went with the truth, just because it was so bloody strange. "This is Theo. He works for the IRS. He had questions about some of my receipts."

Shania, of the colored hair, snorted. "Bullshit."

Dumbass still thought he was dealing with people who played by the rules. "I assure you, it's quite true. I work for the Internal Revenue Service. I have proof. Let me show you my badge." Theo went to reach for the wallet.

"Keep your hands where I can see them!" Shania barked.

Even he understood that command. He raised his arms. "You can look for yourself if you'd like. Back pocket."

The offer resulted in Shania pawing at Theo, who did nothing to evade the groping. Melly scowled rather than do what her lioness suggested, whacking those straying hands away from Theo.

Usually a good sharer, Melly would loan her last clean pair of undies, split a decadent caramel sundae, even let a biatch drive her bike, but she couldn't help a low rumbling growl as Shania touched the man bearing her scent.

If you wanted to make things clear, you should bite him. The suggestion from her feline side had her blinking in shock, and thus she only barely registered Shania's next words.

"Holy shit, he does have a badge."

Shania squinted at the emblem before handing it to Jenny. Jenny bit into it as if she could tell if it was legit. Whereas Barney ignored them all while he played on his phone.

"You're fucking the IRS," snickered Shania. "I guess that's one way to pay less taxes."

"Actually, Theo and I met because of a certain issue with my annual return," Melly hedged.

"And now you're dragging him into a life of crime. How romantic," Jenny said with a sigh.

Less romantic and more crazy. Why had she agreed to this?

Oh yeah, wiping the slate clean at the government bureau.

Apparently thinking everything was chunky-cheese perfect—the curd kind, warm from the vat, being the best —Theo thought he'd just put that other foot in his mouth. "Now that you're satisfied as to my credentials, I am formally requesting in my capacity as an agent for our federal government to meet the person who allegedly sold Ms. Goldeneyes military grade armaments."

"He's requesting." Jenny almost choked. The laughter was well deserved.

Whereas Shania narrowed her gaze. "Whatever Ms. Goldeneyes is claiming is false. No military weapons here."

He eyed the gun in Shania's hands. "Really?"

"Have you actually seen these supposed guns and stuff the feline ho bought?" Shania slipped, or didn't. The "didn't" part being of more concern, as it meant she knew Theo wouldn't be walking out of there alive.

"As a matter of fact, no, I didn't," Theo admitted. "But despite the irregularity of the invoice, there appears to be some truth in her claims, because here you are. Doing your best to avoid answering questions."

"What questions? You haven't really asked any yet," Shania taunted.

Melly craved some buttered popcorn as she waited for the next stupidity to come out of her strait-laced Theo's mouth. He took "by the book" way too literally.

"Are you or your employer selling weapons and other accoutrements? And if yes, have you been submitting the proper taxes for the revenues collected?"

"You've got to be joking." Shania's jaw dropped. "No one is that dumb that they would..." Her voice trailed off, and her gaze narrowed, suspicion spiking in her. "You're wearing a wire, ain't you?"

"I watched him dress. He doesn't have one," Melly stated, knowing and not liking where this was going.

Shania knew it, too, damn that twat. "Says you." Shania poked at him with the barrel of her gun. "I wanna see and make sure. Strip and hand your clothes to Jenny."

Melly moved toe to toe with the hyena girl in barely a heartbeat. The scent of Shania's amusement surrounded her in a musk, which enflamed.

Her lioness paced within, demanding they make the woman pay for her insolence. Disrespecting her was an insult to the pride.

Theo placed a hand on her arm. "It's fine. I can show them I'm not wearing anything." The bastard, obviously eager to strip for an audience, slipped off his coat then his shirt while Melly tapped her foot and crossed her arms in agitation.

There was much ogling of Theo's upper body. For a human, he had a more-than-fine physique.

"Keep going," Shania ordered.

Melly's jealously coiled her hands into fists, and she rocked up onto the balls of her feet. She would deal with Shania first, then Jenny, leaving Barney for last.

Never mind her orders from the king. The need to protect Theo overwhelmed everything.

When Theo's hands went to the waistband of his pants, Barney finally stepped in. "Keep the pants on, bud. You aren't wired, and even if you were, it's not like anyone can hear the signal. Where we're going, no one will find you."

The annoyance in her eased as Theo dressed, calm as could be, which made no sense. A man like him—nerdy, in a suit and glasses, a pencil pusher by trade—should have been shaking in his loafers.

She'd brought a man in loafers to the tunnels.

What was wrong with her?

Nothing a good bite won't fix.

Rawrgh.

CHAPTER NINE

Melly scowled something fierce. She looked like she wanted to bite his head off. Probably thought him the biggest idiot, too. Yet the moment Theodore encountered the trio that greeted them with guns, he'd known he had to be bold. How else would he get close enough to see for himself the layers to this underground operation?

Literally underground. The subbasement opened into a series of tunnels with occasional ladders going up, even more going down. Down into the dark bowels where the light of day never penetrated.

Terrifying and yet exhilarating all at once. He, Theodore Loomer, the Ice Man with the highest dollar count when it came to collecting owed taxes, was heading into danger. He'd lost count of the people they'd encountered. They were armed with guns and, in a few cases, long knives. Might even be swords.

He'd left the rules behind and entered a lawless

place where he could end up hurt or killed. It was hard to wrap his mind around the fact that Melly, she of the sweet taste and passionate noises, had actually been here before. Exactly what kind of woman was she?

The kind to make him act for his own pleasure rather than for his work. That didn't usually happen. He couldn't let it happen, not with this being such a big case. He couldn't afford to be distracted, which was why he needed to get a bead on this Marney person.

The trail went up and down and backtracked, too, by his estimation. The obfuscation method worked quite well. He was lost.

Yet oddly he didn't worry. Keeping cool was his thing. Ice cold. It disarmed people more than any blustering or posturing.

He knew they'd arrived at their destination by the doorway trimmed in blinking Christmas lights with extra guards stationed outside. Sparkling and bright, the lights only served to showcase the damp stone walls. Of true interest, though, was how his allergies remained calm. He didn't do well with musty scents. They usually clogged his sinuses, but he remained clear. Remarkably un-tickly, too.

Perhaps a sign he was improving?

Entering behind Shania, he was taken aback at the sight that greeted him. For one thing, they'd obviously left the sewers behind. While he'd seen signs of habitation during their travels—curtains hung over passages, mattresses surrounded by piles of belongings—he'd not expected to find a town.

The giant cavern, lit with hundreds of strings of lights, was a motley medley of natural stone hollowed out by water and time, along with a ramshackle assembly of shacks. Some were made of corrugated metal sheets riveted together. Others were slats of wood, probably from left-over pallets, nailed into place. Even cardboard had its uses, a few of the lopsided huts made from layers of the thick paper, the surface of it damp and moldy.

If he weren't actually experiencing it, he would have thought it was a movie set with a wild sense of imagination. He'd seen grunge and punk before. He was acquainted with skater types. But the people he encountered here were all that and more. Some wore headbands with furry ears that peeped through their hair. Others had skin tattooed with scales and wore contact lenses that made their eyes appear yellow and slitted. One guy even had his tongue surgically narrowed and split. It almost made Theodore shudder as he went past.

He would never understand why some people chose to change their bodies into something that wasn't human. But he wasn't here to judge or even care how they chose to look. The case he'd been assigned had just exploded. He'd wager not one inhabitant of this underground city paid taxes. He'd just made the discovery of the year, maybe even the decade.

Their arrival engendered some curious looks, mostly aimed at him. He was a tad overdressed, and yet he refused to arrive dressed as someone else. He would never blend in. He could never pull off the tight pants and badass look Melly so casually adopted.

It suited her current expression of angry scowl. She glared left and right, and people avoided her gaze. Almost as if they feared her.

Ridiculous. She was sweet and kind—until they got naked and had sex. Then she was aggressive and demanding. Actually, now that he thought of it, she was bossy when dressed, too.

Their escort led them to an area in the center of the makeshift town. The clearing held nothing but a throne. Of sorts. It towered several feet off the ground, an impressive monument made of junk. Yet despite the use of obvious castoffs, it was nonetheless a work of art. The recycled parts blended to create an impressive seat. They stopped at its base, and he eyed the person perched on top.

They wore a red sequined dress from which cleavage spilled, the valley deep and hairy. The waist was cinched tight via a corset, creating an extreme hourglass shape. The hairy legs peeking from the hem of the skirt ended in combat boots, and while bald, they had a full beard framing a square face. From the lush beard peeked bright red lipstick. The lashes on the mismatched eyes were thick. The gaze assessing. The voice rising and falling when they spoke. "Well, well, what did my bitch drag in?"

Melly tucked her thumbs in the loops of her pants and rocked on her heels. "Hello, Marney."

"If it isn't little Goldie's cub."

"I have a name. Which you know."

Marney smiled. A single silver tooth gleamed amidst sharp-tipped white ones. "Names are for friends. Friends don't bring the government into secret places."

"They do when the IRS is breathing hard down their neck."

"And why is it that you drew their attention? Hmmm?" Marney tapped the arm of the throne. "Rumor has it someone created a paper trail of our transactions."

"Only because I was getting audited," Melly grumbled.

Theodore cast her a startled glance. "You faked them?"

"Yes and no. The purchases were real, and once I knew you were coming, I just put them on paper."

"Exposing me!" Marney declared.

"I did not!" Melly hotly retorted. "I made sure your name and address weren't on the receipt."

"And yet here you are. With the IRS."

"If you haven't been filing your taxes but want to come clean, we might be able to make a deal," Theo offered.

"And what makes you think that I haven't been paying?" Marney teased. "Did you just take one look at me and make assumptions? Isn't that just like one of your kind." The insult was a low growl.

"Actually, I made the assumption before even

meeting you based on the fact you're selling illegal weapons."

"Says who?" Marney flicked their gaze to Melly. "Ah yes, I guess we know who ratted me out."

"You did tell me last time I was here to recommend you to my friends."

"Aren't you just a mouthy cunt today. Have you forgotten who you're dealing with?"

"Hard to forget when you're wearing my aunt's hand-me-downs."

Marney half rose, rage contorting their face.

Theodore stepped in before he realized he was even doing it. "I think we should calm down here."

"You need to be quiet." Heavily kohled eyes lasered in on him. "I'm not talking to you."

"Actually, you are, because I'm the one you've got a problem with. Not Melly."

"You are an inconvenience that I'm about to deal with." Marney snapped fingers tipped in sharpened red nails. "Handle him."

"No!" Melly shouted. "Leave him alone."

"You know I can't."

"He knows nothing," she said.

"He knows enough to cause trouble. You're lucky I owe your king a favor, or you'd be sharing his fate."

Melly's lips compressed. "Speaking of favors—"

"Let me guess, you want to save your boy toy." Marney eyed Theodore. "I can't give you that, but I can arrange one last tryst on the condition you perform for an audience." Marney's smile proved lascivious.

"I don't think so," Melly snapped. "What's it going to take for me to walk out of here with him?"

"What are you willing to give up, Goldie cub?"

Theodore frowned as he said, "What are you doing?"

"Bargaining for your life, idiot. I should have never brought you here. Don't worry. I'm going to fix this and get you out of here."

"To go where? There's nowhere safe for him now that he's been marked," Marney taunted.

"I know places," Melly muttered.

"Look at you, rebelling not only against me but against the wishes of your king." Marney shook their head, and the earrings swung. "I'd admire it if you'd not been so foolish. If you wanted to keep him alive, you should have never told him about me."

"I won't let you kill him." Melly stood in front of him as if she could be his shield.

She truly thought she could protect him. Little did she know he hadn't come unprepared. "No one is dying here today," he stated with assurance. "So long as no one resists arrest."

The words saw silence descend in a large radius around them.

Then Marney laughed. "You? Arrest us? With what army?"

His watch buzzed. The signal. He stood a little straighter. "Attention underground citizens. I am Special Agent Theodore Loomer, and I must inform you that you are officially under arrest for domestic terrorism, including, but not limited to, the selling and provisioning of illegal arms and tax evasion. On your knees, hands over your head, and cooperate if you want to bargain for leniency."

Now, it was true Theo had not been on very many big raids. Actually, this was his first one, but he didn't expect what followed.

Laughter.

So much laughter.

Even worse, the expected reinforcements didn't come pouring in.

He took a chance and flipped his watch to read it. The single message: Almost there.

Bloody incompetents unable to follow a time schedule. Worse, this meant he was on his own, surrounded by guns and people looking more animal-istic by the second. Had Marney always had that serpentine cast to their features?

He glanced at Melly, wishing he'd left her upstairs while he handled business down here. "I'm sorry for what you're about to see."

"You're sorry?" she practically choked. More than likely in fear. "You idiot, they're going to tear you apart."

Like many people, she thought the suit and glasses rendered him helpless. He'd show her. Show them all. Hopefully show them long enough for his backup to arrive.

"Stand behind me. I've got this." He slipped off his

jacket and rolled up his sleeves, which only served to increase the laughter.

"I should have knocked you out again," Melly muttered. "Marney. Let's talk about this."

"Is this where you grovel and apologize? Maybe shove your tongue up my ass?" Marney stood and tugged on the dress, pulling it over the knees.

"Actually," Melly drawled, "I was going to ask if you preferred to die slowly or quickly. Personally, I like slow. It's got more of that lasting effect, but given we've been business friends a while, I could be talked into quick."

The bravado in Melly's words impressed him. But what did she expect to do against these thugs?

"When I say go, hide behind something." His wrist buzzed again: 30 *secs*.

Totally doable so long as no one started shooting at him first. He needed to stall just a little bit longer.

"I don't think you heard me the first time. My name is Special Agent Theodore Loomer, and I am part of the Criminal Investigative Branch of the IRS working in conjunction with the ATF. Put down your weapons and prepare to be arrested." He did things by the books.

Predictably, the criminals didn't listen.

"Kill him!" was the reply.

"You idiot!" was what Melly exclaimed.

As weapons came to bear, his mind whirred. Help was seconds away. Given he doubted they'd shoot the boss, he did the only thing he could. He dove at the throne and grabbed Marney's ankles. He yanked as hard as he could, the surprise of his act dragging them down and causing them both to fall to the floor.

Marney rose with a growl. The dress strained at the seams, and the corset strings snapped one by one.

Theodore punched, fist landing on Marney's chin. Their head snapped back. Before Marney could recover, Theodore dove and wrapped his arm around their torso, taking them both back to the ground. Grappling proved difficult, as the skin he tried to grip rippled oddly. A harsh hiss emerged from Marney as they thrashed.

Rolling on the floor, slamming into legs, he heard the yelled, "I can't shoot. He's in the way."

Exactly how he'd planned. There was screaming, some of it quite strident, and odd snarling, too. He could have sworn he saw Melly leap over him at one point, her hands extended as if they'd become claws, the backs of them furry—probably a trick of the light. As were the sideburns and glowing eyes.

He struggled with Marney, who was freakishly strong and ended up pinning Theodore beneath them. Theodore got worried as Marney leered over him, and then relief hit as a familiar voice shouted, "ATF! You are all under arrest. On your knees, hands on your heads, and don't move!"

Marney's snarl turned to confusion then annoyance, whereas Theodore grinned. "I told you not to resist arrest."

He stood as Maverick arrived in full tactical gear

and pointed to the quivering body at his feet. "Arrest this person for arms trafficking, attempted murder, and tax evasion."

Maverick beamed. "I'll be damned, Loomer. You actually managed to crack the illegal arms group. Good job."

"I couldn't have done it without my informant," he admitted.

A woman who screamed, "Don't you touch me, human."

He turned and saw Melly scowling as two armed agents approached, holding out cuffs.

"Don't arrest her," he yelled, "She's with me."

"Said no woman ever," mumbled someone at his back.

He turned a cold gaze on the agent, who at least had the decency to look sheepish. But he was right. Under normal circumstances, a woman like Melly would never go for a guy like him and not just because they were opposites.

As she stalked toward Theodore, her eyes regarded him with suspicion. Narrowed and assessing. Judging him and probably finding him wanting. "You're not IRS."

"I am, but of a more elevated position than I might have indicated."

"Meaning what?"

"I am a Criminal Investigator tasked with seeking out evidence of fraud, not limited to tax evasion, although that is my specialty."

"You're one of the big guns in the bureau?" She gaped. "You used me!"

He had, and when she was just a name on a piece of paper, he hadn't cared. But now he felt guilt. "I'm sorry. I couldn't tell you what I had planned."

"I guess not." To his surprise she began to laugh, hard and deep. "Oh, am I ever going to hear about this from the boss. Not to mention the fact you're still alive." She slewed her gaze toward him then the agents rounding up those who hadn't managed to flee when the raid occurred. "How did you lead them to Marney, anyhow? Are you bugged?"

"Yes. With a transmitter stronger than the stuff available to the public." He held up his wrist and shook his watch.

"Damn, that's James Bondish. And hot." She shook her head. "Doesn't change the fact you lied to me."

"You did, too," he countered.

"Yeah, but you did it so you could get close to me as a way to arrest Marney. Which means I guess we're done." Her lips turned down as if she felt sorrow at the thought.

He almost told her the real truth, that she and her friends were his mission, but that would involve betraying the bureau. Did it really matter given he'd already compromised his morals by sleeping with her?

His own discomfiture might explain why he blurted out, "They don't need me anymore here. What do you say we go back to my place and shower?"

CHAPTER TEN

G iven sticking around while humans arrested shifters—something she had a hand in—didn't appeal, Melly didn't argue with Theo. A man who was more of a stranger than expected.

He'd managed to surprise her. She'd thought she'd had him pegged, and yet he turned out to not be who and what she thought. For one, he wasn't a pencil-pushing nerd. He was a sooper-seekrit agent. Totally hot. Which was how she'd spin it when the biatches thought to mock her.

However, she'd need a better plan for Arik. He'd flip when he realized what had happened. She was supposed to eliminate a threat. Instead she'd inadvertently exposed them to a huge one.

What if Marney and the others talked? Or did something stupid, say like shift while in custody? What if they pointed fingers at other shifter groups in the hopes of minimizing their time in jail?

The ride was accomplished mostly in silence, probably because he didn't know how to apologize for his lying. He could have told her he'd called in SWAT. Or at the least gotten her a cool bulletproof vest.

He knew enough to apologize as they pulled into his garage. "I am sorry I couldn't tell you."

"It's okay." Because she had her own secrets. "But it will cost you."

"How much?" he asked.

"Your tongue is going to be so sore when you're done apologizing."

For a moment he looked taken aback, and then he smiled. "I shall do my best."

The moment they entered his place, he drew her into his arms for a kiss.

A part of her knew he hoped to distract her. To make her forget what he'd done. But knowing didn't stop her from indulging in passion. She kissed him as if she'd devour him whole. He embraced her just as hard.

There was no hesitation, no shyness. He knew what he wanted, and he took it. This time, her back was the one to hit the wall. His body leaned heavily into hers, and she enjoyed it. Loved it. Creamed herself a bit when he got impatient with her pants and yanked hard enough to pop the laces. Laces that had survived her half shift in the underground and were weak now, but still, it was hot that he was so frantic.

It didn't take much after the pants were gone to denude her. This time, she didn't have to climb his body because he grabbed her by the waist and lifted.

He shoved into her the moment the tip of him found that wet spot.

Thrust into her hard. And she loved it. Loved each pounding stroke. The way he claimed her, intent and powerful. A low growl building in him. A rumble that belonged to no beast and yet fit right in.

What was it about him? Why did she want him so much?

After sex, being a right gentleman, he made her food. Lots of it. Pancakes, bacon, sausage, fruit, whipped cream, and real maple syrup. Liquid gold. She was still mad Arik shut down their plans to smuggle it. She'd even had charts showing how rare real syrup was and how much it could fetch on the sweet tooth market. Arik especially didn't approve the plan to burn down trees in Canada to ensure the few sugar bush companies in the USA that had sap-producing trees quadrupled in value. A shame since she'd bought shares.

They screwed again on the kitchen counter. Some of that syrup might have been involved. A hot shower got rid of the stickiness when they were done. By then the wee hours approached, so they went to bed.

Being a man, he passed out, snuggling her. Weirdest thing ever.

Pleasant, too. She'd never been one for the pile of bodies when it came to sleep. She liked her space, especially if it consisted of a pillow in a puddle of sunlight.

Spooning with Theo reminded her of sunbathing. Warm and comfy. She didn't want to leave. She had to.

It took a slight bit of sly maneuvering to get out of his embrace. She didn't stop for clothes but padded out of his bedroom to stand by the door of the room beside it. The one she'd yet to see. What did he hide in here? She now regretted not checking it out earlier. She might have realized his plan sooner.

Although she would have still slept with him. She just hated being in the dark. A true hacker should always be one step ahead.

The handle had a lock and wouldn't open no matter how much she jiggled and pulled, foot braced on the panel as she tried to snap it.

"Looking for something?"

She jumped. High enough she could have touched the ceiling and stuck to it with her claws. Instead she landed on her feet and tried to look casual while naked. "Hey, Poindexter."

Not exactly the right kind of nickname at the moment given he'd eschewed the glasses and had only put on his boxers. The rest of him was naked yumminess.

He crossed his arms, making himself even more distracting. "Any reason why you're trying to break into my office?"

"Is that what it is?" she asked. "Because for all I know it's an abattoir where you cut up your victims."

"I am not even dignifying that with an answer."

"Fine, then answer this, why keep it locked if you live alone?"

"Nosy overnight guests."

Rather than deny it, she wagged a finger at him. "I have a right to be nosy. You've been hiding things from me."

"I have. I'm allowed my secrets, like you're allowed yours."

"I have no secrets."

He arched a brow. "I'm surprised your nose didn't grow at that whopper of a lie."

"What's that supposed to mean? Why would my nose get big?" She touched it.

"I was referencing Pinocchio. The puppet who came to life."

She kept her face placid to screw with him. "Who?"

"Forget it. It's just a literary children's classic."

"My mom read me fashion magazines as a child. And you're trying to distract me. I want to see." She jabbed a finger at him.

"Why do you need to see inside my office?'" He leaned against the wall, and his arms slipped down, revealing a chest more muscled than a geek had a right to. Tempting. So very, very tempting.

She kept her focus on him, not the insistent throb between her legs. "Because you owe me. I want to know who you are."

"I thought we were done with introductions."

"Are we? Because there's no way you're that clean. Every single search came up with nothing."

"And just who is ordering me investigated?"

As if she'd explain she was the pride's resident hacker. First day they'd met, she'd run him through her databases and not gotten a single interesting ping. Could he really be that straight-laced? "The pride always runs background checks on outsiders. Thorough ones. You checked out."

"Which is a good thing."

"No one is that perfect."

That brought a grin. "Am I supposed to apologize?"

"Who are you really? Because the IRS doesn't have a badass division."

He arched a brow. "No, but we do have access to other government agencies. Be that as it may, despite what you saw during the raid, I am employed by the Internal Revenue Service. The badge is real."

She waved a hand. "Fine, maybe you are really working for them. But you're also more than that. I saw what you did last night."

"My job?"

"You kicked some serious butt."

"I wrestled one person, and not very well. I barely held on to Marney."

"Which is more than people usually manage." She pursed her lips and finally asked the thing she worried about most. "Do you have more secrets?" She really wanted to hear him say that was it. That he had nothing more to hide.

Instead, he hung his head. "The raid on the arms dealer, while a bonus, wasn't the real reason I met with you and some of your friends." Guilt flushed his cheeks.

"You mean there's more?" Her heart began to race. Surely, he didn't know her secret. But she had to know for sure. "Given your interest in me and my family, I'm guessing you're thinking the Pride Group is up to no good."

"Actually, we know for a fact you're breaking laws," was his reply. He grasped the knob to the locked room. It clicked.

"How did you unlock it?"

"Biometrics," he explained as he opened the door.

She was still blinking at the technology not commonly yet in use when she saw what hid in the other room.

"Oh no," she mumbled.

She stepped inside and looked around at the computer equipment, the pictures tacked to the wall. Images not just of her but her family, friends, and more than a few lions.

With a nervous laugh, she pointed to them. "I thought you were allergic to cats."

"I am. Those giants you've got hiding there probably explain my sinus issues whenever I visit that damned condominium. How long has your boss been dealing in exotic pets? Where is he getting them from? Who is he selling them to?"

She almost choked at his misassumption. "You think he's selling them on the black market?"

"Selling, trading, doesn't matter. It's illegal and obviously how he's funding his operations."

The relief made her laugh hard but not forever. Reality set in.

"You've been spying on us." Not just electronic-funds spying but honest to goodness cameras and taking observational notes spying.

This was bad.

"I was assigned to investigate the origin of Pride Enterprises' wealth."

"So the story about coming after me for taxes and offering me a deal..."

"Was a sham to try and get you to spill possible connections to the money. Although when you told me about the guns, I did get sidetracked."

"Angling for a bonus," she muttered.

"Doing my job."

"We're not doing anything illegal."

"That says otherwise." He pointed to the darker-furred lioness sunbathing on the rooftop in one of the images.

Melly hadn't been in the mood to sun in the enclosed gazebo that day. The mirrored windows weren't the same as direct sunlight.

Arik would be pissed.

"Trust me when I tell you that you don't want to tell anyone about this," she declared.

"It's too late. If you might allow me a pun, the kitty is out of the bag. However, if you testify against your boss, I might be able to get you a reduced sentence."

"You'd turn me in?"

"I don't want to." He did appear torn—but pigheaded. "However, I can't exactly shield you unless you agree to help."

"Oh, Theo." She sighed, moving close to him. She peeked up at her lover.

Such a dear sweet man. It hurt her more than him to smack him hard enough to knock his ass out.

CHAPTER ELEVEN

"You did what?" Arik bellowed.

Melly rubbed the toe of her sneaker on his carpet and couldn't meet her king's gaze. "I didn't know what else to do. He was going to arrest us for illegal animal trading."

"With no evidence but a few pictures? My lawyers would have demolished his case. Instead, you knocked the guy out and brought him here." Arik pointed to Theo, hands bound, head covered in a hood, gently placed on the couch in Arik's office.

Boy had that caused some amusement when she arrived and pulled Theo's body out of the trunk. Damned biatches, standing around laughing instead of helping. Tossing remarks like, "Melly's so desperate she has to kidnap a man."

"I panicked," she admitted.

"And now you have to fix it."

"Meaning what?" she asked.

"Make it look like an accident." Arik appeared quite stern.

"What?" she squeaked.

"A fire should do it."

"I am not killing him." She couldn't.

"Obviously. Given the situation, the last thing we want is to draw more notice. Which means we have to be more subtle." Arik eyed Theo.

"How is a fire subtle?"

"Because the cause can be as simple as a pot on the stove going up in flame. Or maybe a cigarette that fell on the couch."

"He doesn't smoke."

He waved a hand. "The how of it is less important so long as it results in the complete destruction of his apartment. We can wipe all the electronic trails, but we need anything he's printed out to be destroyed."

"What of his office? Won't they have copies, too?"

"Not for long," was Arik's grim proclamation.

"After we burn his apartment, what happens to Theo?"

"I'll have my hackers devise a suitable disgrace to keep him busy. Perhaps corporate espionage so he serves time in a white collar institution."

"You can't do that. He didn't do anything wrong." The guy was just doing his job.

"He might not have meant to, and yet he's a danger to us. Keep in mind if we can't neutralize him in a humane fashion, then we'll have to resort to more permanent methods."

"I don't want him to die," she admitted, her head hung in shame.

Arik's tone softened. "And knowing that now I am trying to help keep him from ending up as another body buried in the woods. You really should have spoken up before that debacle with Marney."

Her nose wrinkled. "Sorry about that."

"Don't be. We both made mistakes. I could have done something about the raid when word came through on our channels but didn't."

Her lips rounded. "You knew the SWAT folk were coming?"

"Only barely. I didn't have time to stop it, but I did manage to spring those arrested."

"They've already escaped?"

"Yes, with a little help. Now Marney and company are the ones who owe me a favor." He grinned.

"That's sly."

"I know."

She sighed. "I feel like such an idiot. I never even suspected he was playing me. You'd think I'd have no problem saying, 'off with his head.'" She'd gutted people for less.

"You grew fond of the human. It happens. I should know given I married one. But keep in mind the safety of the pride is more important than any one person."

She knew that and had never balked at eliminating threats in the past. But those people weren't Theo. "I'll do better."

"I know you will. Given all that's happened, I

think it's time we left the city for a countryside retreat a bit earlier than expected. Let things die down."

"I'll go right after I deal with Theo." She glanced at him, still unconscious on the couch.

"Speaking of dealing, use this." Arik reached into a drawer and removed a plastic case.

"What is that?"

He flipped it open to reveal several vials and a syringe inside. "We've been testing a serum in the lab. It's experimental but so far seemingly effective."

"What's it do?"

"Scrambles short-term memories. A few days up to a week. More than enough for him to forget ever coming here or even what he might think he saw in the sewers."

"He wasn't the only one there. Are you going to dose all the agents?"

He shook his head. "No need. By now, they've been treated for sewer gas poisoning, a side effect being hallucinations."

"What of those captured?" More than a few didn't look human.

"Odd how their pictures were lost during their escape, and don't you know you can do anything with plastic surgery these days?"

The boss had thought of everything. She took the case with the drug from him.

"You're sure Theo won't remember anything?" she asked.

"Even if he does recall, it will be fuzzy and filled with holes."

Setting the perfect stage. He wouldn't remember what was real or not, and who would believe him? He might not even recall meeting her.

For the best.

It still made her sad, especially as she pulled the hood off and saw him awake and eyeing her.

"Don't do it," he said. "I can help you."

"You can help me by forgetting." Or else she'd have to hunt him down and handle it.

"I don't want to forget you," he blurted out, and she knew it was true by the color spotting his cheeks.

"I don't have a choice. You could ruin everything."

"Let me protect you."

He still didn't understand that the needle she jabbed into his arm was about protecting *him*.

"I'm sorry." She kissed him as the plunger entered his skin and spilled its secret juice. Kissed him and even felt tears. Her, a badass biatch, crying over a human man.

He growled into her mouth and bucked, kissing her and yet angry at the same time. He bit her lower lip hard enough to draw blood as he muttered, "This isn't over."

Only it was.

He slumped over in a stupor again, and she rubbed her lower lip. The mark barely noticeable and yet...

It's not too late to claim.

Except it was. She'd already injected him. He wouldn't remember her when he woke.

She sniffled again. Damn, maybe she'd caught his allergies.

With a helping hand from a, for once, silent Luna, she got Theo into his car. As they neared his duplex, she saw the flashing lights. Soon enough, even with the windows rolled up, she smelled smoke. Given everyone was already standing a block away, facing the scene of action, she eased Theo from the car, leaning him against a wall. He'd yet to wake up. When he did, he'd be so confused.

She pressed a light kiss to his lips. "Bye, my sweet geek."

I'm going to miss you.

Sad rawr.

CHAPTER TWELVE

H is head throbbed something fierce. Damn Melly for hitting him again. Except it wasn't just a smack to the head. She'd also injected—

The thought almost reached fruition before disappearing. His mind went blank.

Blinking, Theodore realized he was outside, sitting on the sidewalk, and while it was night, lights lit the sky. Red, blue, and white. Emergency vehicles. Turning his head, he saw the firefighters up the street fighting an inferno that licked out of the windows of a building.

I live there.

Lived. He didn't think they'd salvage much. He swallowed, his tongue heavy and thick. He raised his fingers to his scalp, felt the bump. What had happened?

· · ·

SHE HIT ME.

Then she drugged me.

The sluggish thoughts took a while to truly percolate. It was almost as if he wanted to forget it all. As if his mind willfully hid knowledge. Like hell.

He strained to remember, shoved against a fuzzy barrier that collapsed, spilling forth his memories from their first meeting to the raid in the tunnels, the lovemaking and then confronting her in his office about the exotic animal racket. She'd hit him, and then what? The vague recollection of voices refused to coalesce into any sense or shape. He had a faint memory of her kissing him and saying she was sorry before she stuck a needle into his arm. She'd been busy, obviously, given the fire. She wanted to get rid of the evidence, but she hadn't killed him. At least she'd showed him some modicum of respect. That what they shared mattered a little bit at least.

Then again, what did he expect? He'd lied to her. Had led her on in order to complete his task. He'd gone into this like any other job, only it turned out Melly was more than just a mission for him.

He cared for her. Not that she'd ever believe that now. She must hate him. The thought bothered him because he most definitely didn't hate her. She'd actually managed to find the adventure-seeking man within. With her sloppy habits, she gave him a way to make himself useful to her. With her soft moans, she made him feel like the most virile of men.

And he was going to just let her get away?

Glancing at the burning building, he got to his feet and headed in the opposite direction, toward the condo. Problem being once he got there no one would let him in.

The voice on the other end of the intercom denied him. "Sorry, Mr. Loomer, but you're not on the approved guest list."

"Call Melly. Tell her it's Theodore. Theo. She'll let me in."

"Melly's not here. Erm, I mean, we can't confirm or deny her presence in this establishment." The preset phrase emerged by rote.

"That's bullshit." The rare expletive slipped from his lips as his frustration mounted. Surely, she wouldn't be so...what? Undesirous of his presence? She wouldn't even let him explain? He would have never let anything happen to her.

When his attempts to enter failed, he finally resorted to calling the office, which proved a tad frustrating given he'd lost his phone. Or Melly had taken it.

Didn't matter. He bought one with the wallet he'd been allowed to keep. It took a few codes and several transfers before Maverick picked up.

"Loomer! Where have you been? There are some people who want to talk to you about the Lipstick Grenade case."

"The what?"

"The ring you helped us bust has been one we've been trying to stop for years. We kept finding evidence of the weapons but not a clue as to where they were originating. Pity they escaped."

"What?"

"A massive jailbreak the likes of which we've never seen. They all escaped, including the ringleader, Marney, but no matter. We now have names and faces. It won't be long until we see them again."

"About the other case, sir—"

"Don't tell me you're still on that Pride Group thing. Didn't you get my message?"

"What message?"

"The one telling you to drop it. We are no longer interested in the Pride Group."

"But the evidence—"

"Showing improper tax filings has been handled. Returns have been amended, money repaid, and the fines handled."

Theodore closed his eyes and leaned against a brick façade. "It wasn't just about the income tax returns. What of the lions?"

"Weren't real lions. Turns out there's some freaks living in that condominium. Part of some weird sex cult group that likes to dress up and pretend they're wild animals."

"How did you find out?"

"Quite by accident. A call came in that there was a pack of lions on the loose. The cops went to look, but it turned out to be a bunch of folks from that condo dressed in fur. Quite drunk."

It explained the images but not Melly's reaction.

Unless...she was embarrassed because she was part of it.

Now he'd be the first to admit he didn't understand the allure of pretending to be a lion, but if it meant having a chance with Melly, a woman that made the Ice Man melt into a puddle, then... "Listen, sir, I don't suppose I could have a few days off."

"A few days? Hell, take a week. You did good, Loomer. We'll have more work for you since you've proven you can handle the big stuff."

"Really, sir?" He was surprised and pleased.

"Guess we shouldn't be so stingy on our requirements in the future."

Meaning myopic agents could still fill a role. Once the thing he'd longed to hear more than anything, but now he wanted to hear a woman say she'd give him a second chance. The question was, how to get her to listen?

Since no one would let him through the gates and Melly wasn't answering her phone—it went to a voicemail box that roared for a minute then beeped—he infiltrated the grounds of the condominium.

It wasn't rational or smart. It was the most insane thing he'd ever done, yet that didn't stop him. He wore all black, even covered his face. He made it over the wall in between cameras, which wasn't easy. Their security was almost seamless, except in one spot where they'd let a tree grow over the wall, providing a small spot where someone climbing over could not be seen.

He dropped the crate he'd thought to bring and, by

jumping on it, managed to catch the lip of the wall. He only grunted once as he made it onto the top. The branches barely rustled as he dropped into the garden. He traversed the grounds quickly, doing his best to appear like just any other shadow. Proud of his stealth. Everything remained quiet. No alarm.

He'd managed to sneak in undetected.

"LOOK AT THAT IDIOT. Could he be any louder?" Aunt Marissa declared, clucking her tongue.

"I kind of wanna shout 'boo,'" Joan declared.

Marissa, watching the entertaining antics of the human, understood the urge. "We can't. Arik said no doing anything weird. We have to seem normal."

That had Joan snorting. "Normal? That's not likely. Melly's nerd already thinks we're furries." People who liked to dress up in animal costumes and pretend to be those animals, even during sex.

"Better furries than the alternative." They couldn't be caught. The stakes were too high.

"It's embarrassing to the extreme," Joan mumbled.

"I take it your girlfriend saw the news footage."

"She did, and oh boy did she have some questions." Joan sighed.

"He almost tripped on Gunther," Marissa remarked, the black panther quite visible to them but not the night-blind human.

"I say we go furry and say hi."

Marissa shook her head. "We can't draw attention."

"But look at him. He's practically begging us to do something evil. I'll bet if I go giant kitty on him, he pees his pants," Joan said almost hopefully.

"Melly would kill us."

"Melly dumped his ass when she found out he was lying. She won't care."

"Don't be so sure. I think there's something going on between them." She'd seen it that day her niece came barging in to save him. The coveting glint in her eyes, the deadly jealousy in her snarl.

"Melly and a human?" Joan sounded appalled. "Oh, don't wish that on her. You know what will happen."

"Violently loud entertainment? It sounds delicious."

"You're so bad," Joan exclaimed. "She's your niece."

"She is, and I'm wagering she wins." As the human approached the rear of the condo and the utility door tucked behind the large bush, Marissa thumbed her watch and unlocked it.

He slipped inside.

"What are you doing?" Joan asked.

"Take a wild guess."

They exchanged a look. Smiled. It wasn't the kind of grin anyone wanted to be the recipient of.

"I'll get the duct tape," Joan said.

"No time. We need to beat him to her apartment."

ENTERING the unlocked utility door at the back of the condo, he managed to avoid cameras and the night watchman. Even better, the stairwell to Melly's place was empty. His luck was on fire tonight. Just a sign he was doing the right thing.

The next part would be trickier. Having reached her apartment, he was confronted with a locked door. Knocking would just give her a chance to send him away, if she was around. The guard earlier today had said she'd left.

Left to go where? Only one way to find out. A good thing he'd brought his lock picks.

He laid the set on the floor and chose his tools, ignoring the voice in his head that asked him what he was doing. Was he really going to break in? How stalkerish was that?

Sighing, he put away his kit, stood, and raised his fist to knock. Before it could land, the portal swung open and he gaped, not at Melly but at the two women smirking at him, only one of whom he recognized.

"And just what do you think you're doing?" asked the blonde in athletic gear, her hair a smart bob, her voice quite stern.

"Now, Joan, isn't it obvious. He's here to see his sweet Melly," cooed Melly's aunt Marissa.

"Er, hello, Mrs. Vandercoop."

"Please, call me Marissa." Mrs. Vandercoop eyed

him in a way that made him wish for more clothes. Her wink didn't help.

"Is Melly home?" he asked, soldiering through his discomfort.

"No."

"Oh."

He must have let some of his disappointment show because Marissa trilled. "I think someone is horny. I can help you with that if you like."

"Uh, no thank you." He backed away.

The athletic blonde eyed his hand. "What's that you got?"

"Nothing."

Even as he spoke, she snatched it from him and whistled at the contents of the leather wallet. "That's some fine lock-picking gear you've got."

"I wasn't going to use it."

"Then why bring it?"

"Because at first, I wanted to surprise her."

"That's an excuse rapists use." The gaze narrowed.

"I would never!" he huffed.

"Should hope not or we'd eviscerate you and eat your heart." Funny how the toothy smile made it seem like she spoke the truth.

"I just want to talk to her. Explain a misunderstanding we had."

"You mean the one where you're not just an IRS agent but a super-spy agent, too?" Marissa said.

"I'm not a spy. But I am in a position where I can summon task forces to provide backup."

"Which you call in after spying on people and figuring out if they're up to no good," Joan stated. "Po-tay-to, po-tah-to."

"I never meant to lie to her. I had the job before we met," he protested.

"I can't believe she fell for your bullshit. I never knew she could be so gullible." Joan shook her head.

"Now, Joan, don't be mocking my niece for being led by her cootchie. We've had our share of trouble, too, when we let the other set of lips make our decisions. You have to admit, he is pretty." Marissa tapped his cheek.

"If you like that sort. I prefer mine without the dangly bits in the middle."

"If I could just talk to her—" he began.

"Talk? Ha! Is that what you call it?" Joan snickered.

"I think we should give the man what he wants," Marissa declared, taking a step toward him.

"I thought you told me not to get the duct tape." The glance Joan tossed Marissa held annoyance.

"We won't need it because he's going to come with us nicely, aren't you?" Marissa's gazed narrowed on him

He retreated a few paces down the hall. "Maybe I'll come back to talk to her another time."

"It's now or never. But I recommend now while she still thinks of you fondly. Give her a bit of time to mull things over and I'm sure she'll come to hate you."

"I never meant to hurt her."

"Hurt Melly?" More laughter. "Honey, it's a surprise you're still alive. Melly doesn't usually handle betrayal that well. I still remember what she did to Gary the tiger when he told her there was no more of Aunt Mary's apple pie. When she found the piece he'd hidden in the fridge, well...let's just say he still faints at the sight of a ripe apple. But you're not family. She wouldn't be as nice to you."

"Because that's what the pride does. We take care of our own." Joan moved to flank him.

"Melly's not a killer." But he wasn't so sure about her aunt and friend.

"That's where you're wrong, honey." Marissa's tone dropped. "Melly's a hunter through and through. And if the pride gives her a target, she always tracks down her prey."

"Are you prey?" Joan stepped closer.

There was something menacing in their gazes and body language. It occurred to him that perhaps he should leave. Only, when he turned around to either ride the elevator or skip down the stairs, he found himself hemmed in by more women. They'd arrived on silent steps, most of them tawny haired with their skin hues varying in shade, eyes glowing slightly golden with hints of green and brown. Their expressions weren't exactly hostile, and yet his skin prickled and the hair on his nape lifted.

He froze.

One of them with a pierced nose and a shaggy

ponytail smirked. "So this guy is why Melly's been moping."

"He's kind of boring looking," said a woman with a large pregnant belly.

"Maybe she likes peeling him out of his suit. I know I would," said a statuesque redhead.

"They say nerds work harder with their tongues."

The comments were tossed back and forth, some ribald enough to make him blush.

"I think it's cute he came looking for her," said a petite woman.

"Doesn't matter what we think. I say we give the boy what he wants," Mrs. Vandercoop declared. "Anyone up for a kidnapping and a road trip?"

The girl with the piercing held up a roll of tape while the pregnant lady shook a pillowcase.

The problem with having old school chivalry? He couldn't hit a woman, not even a bunch of them intent on subduing him and stuffing him into the back of a van. But then again, why struggle when they were giving him what he wanted?

They were taking him to see Melly.

CHAPTER THIRTEEN

M elly moped. Not just your regular run-of-the-mill kind of mope. She was talking full-on, lip-jutting, stuffing-her-face-eating kind of mope.

She missed Theo. Stupid really given she'd only known him for a few days, but being separated from him was actually physically unpleasant. She just wanted to lie in bed, under the covers, eating potato chips and ignoring the pile of crumbs accumulating in her bed.

The farm—ranch, whatever you wanted to call the massive acreage with its giant house with so many additions it could have rivaled the Winchester Mystery House in California—the many outbuildings, the forest kept stocked with game, the pond with its koi fish and frogs, the river with the trout couldn't distract her for once. She flopped from an inside couch to an outdoor couch. From tree branch to tree swing. Even tossing Kerry from the porch rocker she suddenly wanted didn't do a thing to lift her spirits.

Melly missed her pencil-pushing, muscle-bound, book-quoting geek. It sucked she'd never see him again.

Meow.

Even worse, she mourned his loss alone. Under the influence of the serum, he wouldn't remember her at all. Would never know his brief respite from allergies was because of her. Slipping him the drug hadn't been easy, but she'd managed a dose here and there, because nothing annoyed her more than a man who couldn't get near her.

Even if he weren't prone to sneezing fits around felines, it would have never worked. The man didn't like animals. He was employed by a government that would love to get its hands on her. He didn't have a single flexible bone in his body—especially the one between his legs. So long and hard and...

She clenched her legs tight, and her mood turned even more foul. When some mouthy biatch thought she could get away with asking, "Are you okay?" Melly tossed her into the pond.

And when Aria's husband dared protest? She tossed him in, too. It did nothing to appease her mood.

And then her aunt appeared in all her flamboyant glory, wearing a pantsuit that molded her curves. Her hair was swept into some kind of fancy bun with pieces hanging down. She looked good, especially compared to Melly in her stretched-out and stained track pants and the T-shirt with a pudgy dough boy and the quote, Poke me and die.

Auntie didn't heed the warning. "There's my darling niece. I've been looking for you."

"Why don't you go play in traffic?" Melly snarled.

"I see someone's about to go on her period."

True, but not the reason for her bad mood. She scowled. "Leave me alone."

"Where's the fun in that?"

"You want fun, then why don't you go seduce someone's younger husband?"

A hand with red-tipped nails—an extravagance given it flaked the moment they shifted—fluffed the already bouffant hair. "I have plans to seduce more than one, actually. I hear the bear sleuth has arrived and they're just raring to go."

Ah yes, the impending football match. It must be happening soon and would explain the camper vans and tents that had popped up all over the place. For the next few days, there would be bodies everywhere. Finding a place to sleep would be a challenge for those that didn't arrive early or come prepared.

Given her family connections, Melly rated a spot in the cramped attic with the sloped ceilings. Personally, she thought it was the best place. Access to the roof, her own three-piece bathroom, and a twin-sized bed she didn't have to share. It also didn't have an annoying aunt.

"Don't let me keep you from your home-wrecking plans," she said with a wave of her hand.

"I always have time for you, dear niece." Which could have been construed as a threat. "If you want, I can find you a nice bear to play with."

"I don't need anybody."

"In that case I have implements you can borrow to ease any urges you have."

"Gross." And what did her aunt mean by implements? It sounded more ominous than a vibrator.

"I'll have you know I sterilize my toys better than any medical office."

"Can we stop talking about sex? I don't want sex with a bear or some piece of plastic."

"Don't tell me you're pining over that human you were banging?"

She had to bite back her first retort, which was they'd done more than *banging*. But that would imply he meant something to her. She blew a raspberry. "Please. As if."

Her aunt got a sly look. "Good to know you're done with him."

"Why?" She just had to ask, even knowing she wouldn't like the answer.

"Because he is just my type." Her aunt offered a slow, evil smile. "Corruptible."

Rawr. Before she even knew what she was doing, Melly sprang at her aunt. However, her blind jealousy was no match for a lioness of experience. Auntie moved quickly aside and delivered a blow that sent her flying, tumbling to the ground and then cartwheeling to her feet.

Auntie wasn't done. She gave Melly a few love taps, a head lock, and then a firm spank on the bottom with an admonishment, "Slow, girl. Still too slow. And dumb. Really, coming after me?"

All true. Given Melly had attacked first, she couldn't even be mad. "Sorry."

"I'll forgive you this time." Auntie blew on her nails, checking the polish. "Good thing you're not pining."

Melly brushed herself off. "Just checking your reflexes."

"My body is fine. Why, last night, the man I picked up at the bar said—"

Rather than listen to her aunt discuss her conquests and taunt her for her lack of acuity with men, she moved toward the house. She planned to return to her bed and stare at the ceiling, maybe bat at the mobiles she had suspended from the rafters. Only Aunt Marissa stopped her with a simple statement.

"Before you go, I should get to the real reason I came to find you. Do you want to join us for a hunt?"

For a brief moment, the idea of running through the woods appealed.

Yes. Run. Chase. Hunt. She could use a stretch of her legs and the fresh air of the forest.

But that would require dropping the mope. It seemed too soon. She wanted to mourn the loss of the thing she'd never had but wanted more than she'd realized. "No, thanks."

"Probably for the best given you've gone soft."

"What's that supposed to mean?" Melly whirled.

"Had you taken care of that IRS fellow from the beginning, we wouldn't be in this mess. Really, Melly, consorting outside your kind. What would your mother say?"

Plenty. But she was more interested in the rest of her aunt's words. "What do you mean mess? Arik took care of Theo and his case."

The fire for the physical evidence, a hacking team for the electronic stuff, cleaners for the IRS office, and a drug to make a man forget he'd almost made a lioness purr. Then there was the ridiculous charade to pass them off as furry lovers. They were free and clear.

"We all thought it was over, but lo and behold, your wily little human somehow found the ranch. Why, if I didn't know better, I'd say someone had him brought here and dropped in the woods for sport."

Her eyes widened. It was only two days out from a full moon and even less from a bloody rivalry between two predator groups. "Theo is here?"

"Like I said, a good thing you're done with him." Auntie walked away.

Melly jumped in front of her. "Where is he?"

An assessing gaze held hers. "Why do you care?"

"I don't know," she shouted. The honest truth. The only certainty she could claim was she had to find him.

Protect. Ours. Her feline paced and pushed.

"If you want him that badly, then you better get going. Your IRS fellow is in the woods."

"Where in the woods?" Because they spanned hundreds of acres.

"As if I'm going to make it that easy. You're a huntress. Find him yourself. But because you're my favorite niece, here's a bit of help." From a pocket, Auntie pulled out a sealed plastic baggie. A second later she dangled Theo's tie.

How had she gotten her paws on it?

Melly almost wasted time throttling her aunt for answers, but Auntie would never reveal his location. She was perverse that way. However, Melly knew these woods better than anyone. She'd spent her childhood here, hunting the forest, learning the scents and tracks of every living thing.

As a lioness.

She needed her other half, the speed, the uncanny perception. The clothes came off, shedding in a stream of items on the lawn as she bolted toward the tree line. Her lioness burst free in a shower of fur and fangs and claws. The elation of being in her other form brought forth a roar.

Let it act as a warning. The lioness did not sleep tonight.

Entering the woods, she dropped into tracking mode, filtering smell and sound, noting every breeze and the scents contained in it. She raced, faster than ever before, her heart pounding, driven by adrenaline and fear. What if she was too late? While the hunting of humans was against their laws, sometimes accidents did happen—and sometimes it wasn't an accident, especially when it came to nosy humans who knew too much.

Why had her aunt brought him? Had Arik lied? Was Theo doomed no matter what?

She wouldn't let him be killed. Couldn't.

Because he's ours.

Her lioness stated it as if it were fact. Surely not. Melly understood the problems it would cause. The fighting with her family. The difficulty in making cubs. The fact he wouldn't be able to handle her secret.

The moment she found him all those doubts slipped away. Only one instinct remained. She had to save him, which might not be the easiest task given he was surrounded by bears. At least the man showed enough sense to climb a tree. He appeared a bit frazzled, his glasses askew, but then again, he had cause. He held tight as the tallest grizzly shook the trunk.

Did they not grasp the fact that if Theo fell, he would break?

They are trying to hurt him.

Rawr.

She bounded right into their midst with a loud roar that resulted in the five bears present standing on their back legs and chuffing.

Sassing her? On pride land? Oh hell no.

She approached the biggest one and snarled. Percy, recognizable by scent, backed off. At his retreat, the others gave her space, too. She cast a glance up at the tree. Theo gaped in astonishment. He'd be gaping a whole lot wider in a second because there was no avoiding what had to come next.

Melly shifted into her female shape, naked but unafraid as she faced off against the bears.

"Melly?" Theo sounded confused.

He knew her name? She glanced up at him. "Do you remember me?"

"Of course, I do."

"Like how much do you remember? As in read my name in a file? Or face between my thighs?"

"What the hell are you yammering on about? I know you. How could I forget the woman that knocked me out?" he growled.

He did remember. "I did it for a good reason."

"Care to explain?"

"In a minute. Let me deal with these imbeciles first." Turning her attention back to the bears, she crossed her arms and tapped a foot.

Percy shifted. "I am not an imbecile."

"Hunting a human on pride land?"

"We had permission."

Of course, they did. Her damned aunt.

"We weren't going to eat him," declared a smaller fellow who cupped his groin. "The lady said we could screw with him for a bit and then run him off the property."

"And I am here to tell you it's not okay. Leave him alone."

"Well now, maybe if you'd not interfered, we could have. But you know we can't do that now," Percy replied. "He saw us. He knows." The only reason any shifter had to give to be justified in dealing a killing blow.

So she gave the only reply that would get them to leave Theo alone. "He's my mate."

CHAPTER FOURTEEN

If Theodore thought the strangest part of his day was getting kidnapped by Melly's aunt and dropped in the middle of the woods, he was wrong. So very, very wrong.

He'd wandered around lost for about an hour before coming across the bears lying in a raspberry bush, looking drunk, their snouts smeared in mashed fruit. They'd snapped out of their stupor quick as he tried to retreat and stepped on a tiny branch. Who had ears good enough to hear the tiny crack?

Bears did!

Theodore hightailed it out of there. He thought he'd lost them, but next thing he knew, they were charging from the woods. He had to quickly climb something to get out of reach. Only in retrospect did he remember bears liked trees.

His future as raspberry-smeared bear shit seemed

certain when the lion appeared. No mane, making it a female. Not just any female but Melly.

The lioness turned into the woman he'd been having sex with, which was when he knew this was obviously a dream. And a vivid one, too.

The odd thing about it was the strange fantasy element. Melly as a shapeshifter, the bears, too. Completely wacky given everyone knew only were-wolves had that ability, if one believed in that kind of thing.

The realization this was a dream made it easy for him to shimmy down the tree. He had nothing to fear. The worst-case scenario? He'd wake up.

Melly eyed him cautiously. "Are you okay?"

He wanted to say all kinds of things to her, but they had an audience. Not to mention she was naked and all he wanted to do was...

Fuck it. It was a dream. No one was actually watching, and she had called him her mate. He drew her into his arms, amazed at the way he felt her warm flesh in his dream, the soft pliancy of her mouth. The sharp nip of her teeth on his lip had him drawing in his breath, the pain fleeting, the coppery tang his own. The violence of it only fueled his desire. Made him want more and he bit her right back, mingling their blood, their breath, their passion.

This was why he'd gone to the condo. The way he felt around her. He liked the man he became in her presence.

He liked a lot less the whistling and bear-calling at his back.

"Hot damn, we are getting a live show," someone declared.

"Think we can join in?" asked another.

That got Theodore snarling, "Go away. This is *my* dream."

"Oh, Theo," Melly sighed softly. "You're not dreaming."

"Of course, I am. Lions and bears, then you and your ex. It's my subconscious screwing with me."

"You're awake, Poindexter. Everything you saw is real."

"Impossible." He took a step away from her.

"I assure you it is possible. I'm a shapeshifter. A lioness to be exact."

He shook his head, the denial still strong. "Shapeshifters aren't—"

He never did get to finish that sentence because someone slapped him on the back. It was the big, hairy man that he'd seen before at the restaurant, and he was naked.

"Congrats, mate. Never thought we'd see the day Melly would settle down. And with a human of all things."

There was something kind of disparaging about being referred to in such a manner, but then again, given a moment ago Percy was a giant freaking bear, he wasn't about to say anything about it.

"Shapeshifters are real," Melly admitted, unashamed of her nudity.

Everyone but him was naked. Was it weird to feel overdressed? Then again, given the size of the men who'd gone from bear skin to giants in the flesh, perhaps he needed more layers. The intimidation factor was quite literally huge.

"You're a lion shapeshifter," he repeated. The truth slowly filtered in as things began to make sense. "You're not the only one, meaning the Pride Group was never in the exotic animal trade. And they're not Furries either." At least not in the sense they needed a costume.

"Most of the people in that building are like me."

"Lions?" He glanced at Percy. "But you're bears."

"And damned proud of it." The big man flexed and grinned.

Melly grabbed Theodore's cheeks and forced him to face her. "They're a sleuth living the next state over."

"How many of you are there?" he asked. Because if that whole condo was full of lions...that was a lot of freaking claws and teeth living free instead of in a cage at the zoo. A thought that shamed him the moment it occurred.

"Enough that you really don't want to tell anyone."

"Speaking of telling, how is he your mate if he only just found out?" The smaller guy bounced his gaze between them.

Melly chewed her lip. "I hadn't gotten around to it."

"You didn't get around to a lot of things," Theodore snapped. "Were you ever going to tell me?"

"Tell you how? Hey, Poindexter, I'm a lioness. How would that have gone?" She shook her head. "You weren't ever supposed to know. The serum we injected you with was supposed to take care of your memories. Make you forget me, the case, everything. I guess my aunt kidnapping you ruined the effect."

"What serum?" He rubbed his head. "You know what, I'd rather not know. I went to your condo to talk to you and apologize for hiding the truth from you and ask if you'd give me a chance to make things right. Only it turns out your secret is worse."

"I wouldn't call it worse."

"You're a giant cat."

"I am."

"I'm allergic to cats."

"Are you sure about that? Because you're not sneezing," she pointed out.

"At the moment, but it will come. It always comes," he repeated ominously.

"Don't be so sure of that," she muttered.

"What she means is mated humans often find themselves more resistant to infections. Allergies kind of fall under that umbrella." The tidbit came from a guy who'd at least found a branch with leaves to hold in front of his junk.

"We can't be mated since we're not even dating,"

he said firmly, in direct contrast to what he thought he wanted before he'd been kidnapped.

"Dating." A big snort emerged from Percy. "You have lots to learn, bro."

"And I will be the one to tell him all about it," Melly declared, hooking his arm and trying to pull him away.

But he wasn't ready for her. This.

He yanked free. "No, you won't. If you'd wanted to tell me, you would have instead of ghosting me."

"It was supposed to be for your own good. I was saving your life," she hissed.

"I don't need your help."

"As a matter of fact, you do. Now that you know our secret, you're kind of stuck with us."

"Going to kill me if I don't agree to become your obedient servant?" was his sarcastic retort.

"I won't kill you," she said.

"We will." Percy flexed and punched a fist into his palm.

"Try it, big boy," Theodore threatened, not in the mood for anyone's crap.

"He's feisty," announced another of the naked men. "Pity he plays for the opposite team."

"Touch my man and I will make you sing soprano, Derek," she snarled.

"Children, children, and children all grown up," Mrs. Vandercoop said, suddenly appearing and casting a lascivious eye over Percy, who turned red and tried to cover himself. "Must we bicker?"

"You did this!" Melly snapped, pointing her finger at her aunt.

"Because you were too stubborn to do anything about it yourself. Don't tell me you're actually mad," Mrs. Vandercoop said slyly.

Melly's lips flattened. She looked pissed, but she managed a gritted, "I am going to kill you."

"You are so welcome. I'm glad this has all been cleared up. And just in time for the coin toss to see who gets the ball first for tomorrow's game." Her aunt clapped her hands.

"Last one there has to use the no name brand of toilet paper," shouted Derek, who suddenly shifted in a dizzying display that saw flesh reshaped and turned into fur.

In under a minute, all the bears were gone, leaving him with Melly and a cougar in human clothes

"Now that they're gone, feel free to thank me." Mrs. Vandercoop smirked.

"You should have minded your business," Melly grumbled.

"And missed the entertainment that's about to erupt?" The older woman grinned. "Your mother is going to flip when she finds out."

"You'll be the one running to tell her I guess?" Melly's brow arched.

"Perhaps you'd prefer to do it."

Head bobbing between them, Theodore tried to make sense of the conversation and failed. Nothing was following any straight lines or the truth he thought he knew. He sat down, suddenly overwhelmed by it all.

Melly crouched before him. "I won't let my mother hurt you."

"How about I just don't meet her?"

"As if that's going to happen. You're mated to her daughter, which is a bond that is until death do you part."

"I never agreed to that." Even as the very idea made his pulse pound. Now that he'd gotten over his initial shock, curiosity rose in its place. Melly wasn't a criminal. The case no longer acted as a reason for them to be apart. There was now truth between them—and still so much passion.

"Let's go back to the farm and I'll try to explain everything."

He rubbed his head. "I'd rather we chatted elsewhere." The idea of being surrounded by predators...

"I can't go. Not before the football match tomorrow. It's kind of a tradition."

"Surely they don't need you to be a cheerleader on the sidelines?"

She blinked at him. "Cheer? Oh, my silly Theo. I'm the pride's star running back."

CHAPTER FIFTEEN

Things didn't entirely go as Melly had imagined. Theo wasn't overjoyed to see her. He did, however, take the news of her being a shapeshifter better than expected. Until she actually shifted for the walk back to the house.

He yelped. "Holy jumping Jiminy Crickets."

If she could have laughed, she would have. Instead she sat down and stared at him. Might as well get this part out of the way. It took him a long moment where he stood frozen and watching, and then he reached out a hesitant hand. Finding his nerve, he rubbed the top of her head, stroking her fur and ears, having a natural instinct for what she liked. Soon she was turning into his caress, almost tapping a paw on the ground in pleasure.

"You're soft," he said.

Soft all over.

"And you don't smell bad."

A remark that had her drag her teeth along his arm.

He stilled. "You're pretty?"

She'd accept it even with the hesitancy. This was a lot for him to take in.

When she stood to walk, he kept one hand on her and spoke aloud, "I never had a chance to tell you, but I've missed you. Which is dumb. I know. I mean it's been like what, forty-eight hours since we saw each other? And yet...it felt longer."

Like an eternity.

"I went looking for you at the condo. To promise no more secrets and see if you wanted to maybe see each other."

Her heart pounded, and she almost knocked him down for a head-to-toe lick, but the farm wasn't too far now. She could wait a little bit longer.

"I guess I can understand why you avoided me."

Not out of choice, but she couldn't tell him that yet.

"So what happens now? I get the impression Percy and the others weren't joking about killing me and burying my body somewhere no one would find it."

"Growr."

It startled him, but he understood it wasn't for him. "A good thing I'm not planning to tell anyone about this. And not just because they wouldn't believe me. I won't do anything that hurts you, Melly. You have my word."

She'd wager that word was worth its weight in gold.

He glanced down. "Is it weird that it feels like we were meant to be?"

What do you know? Even humans could feel the hand of fate.

Arriving at the house, no one thought it strange at all that her furry ass had a human following it. If anyone had dared to say a word, things might have gotten clawy, but lips were sealed, and for once, Theo kept his mouth zipped.

Until they reached her room and she shifted. Twice in one day. It left her tired, and she flopped on the bed, naked. "I need a nap."

"I thought I was getting answers."

She peeked at him out of one eye. "I was born this way. My people have existed since the dawn of man. You won't change into an animal, unless it's during sex with me." She winked.

"Only you, right?"

"Were you eyeballing someone else?" she snarled, suddenly awake.

He smiled. "No. Just making sure we're exclusive."

As in a couple.

A mated couple.

That quickly, the fatigue left her, and she crooked a finger. "Come here."

"Are we done talking?"

"For now. I missed you."

He fell on her, his mouth hot and ravenous, his cock hard and ready.

He rode her, and then she rode him. They spent the night making up for the two days they'd spent apart and fell asleep in a tangle of limbs on her small bed.

The door to the attic slammed open, causing them both to jolt. Theo, on the bottom, didn't have to worry about falling out of bed, but lying on top, she didn't have a chance to move before someone grabbed her by the ankle and dangled her in the air.

The joys of being the shortest in a family of tall, blonde giants.

Her mother scowled at her. "So it's true. You've taken up with a human."

"Mated him actually. Mother, meet Theo."

The head of the pride army, known as Goldie the killer, sneered. "There's no point in learning his name given he won't be living past breakfast."

CHAPTER SIXTEEN

"You will not kill him, Mommy!" Melly shouted, still dangling from her mother's hand.

Theodore caught up quickly on the situation but had no idea what to do about it. There was something a little daunting about a woman who outsized a man and made no bones about her dislike of him.

"I am head of this family. I will do what has to be done."

"He's my mate!" Melly twisted and ended up on her feet, but that didn't stop the epic row with her mother.

About him.

"Either you get rid of him, or I will!" Mrs. Gold-eneyes declared.

"Theo's not going anywhere. I claimed him. Did you hear me? Claimed. Him. He's mine."

In other circumstances he would have argued the

fact that no own actually owned him, but this seemed a good situation to try keeping quiet.

"He's *human*." Again, with that disparaging note.

"I don't care." A vehement reply that warmed him and not just the parts blushing because he was naked under the sheets.

He rolled out of the bed and wrapped the sheet sarong style. The fight continued.

"How do I know you're not simply claiming him to embarrass me?"

"If I want to embarrass you, I will."

"If he's yours, prove it."

"I know you can smell my mark."

"Anyone can bite a human. I want proof it is fate."

"Seriously? Whatever. Let's have at it. What will make you happy?"

Mrs. Goldeneyes tapped her lip as if in thought and her gaze turned cold and calculating. "Make sure the pride wins the football match today."

For some reason this brought laughter bubbling to Melly's lips. "Is that all? Piece of cake. We win every year."

"So you agree?" Mrs. Goldeneyes seemed pleased with the reply.

"I agree. I win and you leave me and Theo alone."

"Deal. But if you lose..." No need to finish that ominous sentence.

"Pride won't just win. We'll do it by at least two touchdowns," Melly boldly declared before Theodore could jump in.

He had a feeling she'd walked into a trap, and the smirk on Mrs. Goldeneyes' face confirmed it a moment later.

"Excellent. I'll be watching from the stands. Oh, and by the way, I guess now would be a good time to mention your star quarterback is throwing up in the main floor bathroom. Something about a batch of bad moonshine."

Melly's smile faded. "Patricia is out? That's fine. We still have Lily."

"Actually, she's not going to make it. Her audition for that television spot is today. Don't worry, you still have Robin."

At Melly's groan he could only discern that as a bad thing.

"Is Robin not any good as a QB?" he queried.

"Oh, she's fine. Problem is we always lose at least one QB a game. We tend to play rough," she explained.

He got to see how rough within two hours of the massive breakfast being served. He'd never seen such a mound of pancakes—per plate. When he ate only two of the eight stack and declared himself full, forks came stabbing for the rest. As for the last piece of bacon he couldn't manage, there was definite jealousy in more than one gaze as he fed it to Melly.

There was much good-natured jibing and more than one pointed stare his way, but other than an initial comment—"Ah look, the pride got themselves a dorky mascot"—everyone steered clear of him.

It was only as Melly left to get ready for the match he got worried. Mostly because her mother pounced him, literally, dropping from a porch roof, grabbing his arm, and declaring, "You will sit with me. That way if the pride loses, I won't have to waste time hunting you down."

There was no way to call for help, and even if he could, what would he say? *Hi, can you come rescue me from shapeshifters that are planning to kill me if the lions lose to the bears?* No one would ever believe him. The NFL versions of those teams weren't even playing this weekend!

The field of play was surrounded by a motley collection of odd people and seating. Lawn chairs, cushions, blankets, even a few picnic tables carted over by golden-haired people. So much golden hair all around. Melly's dark hair stood out in many respects. Odd how her lioness didn't match the hue.

Odder still how he was already accepting this facet of her. He kind of looked forward to learning more because obviously shapeshifters had existed for some time and managed to coexist with humanity.

"You look serious, human. Are you contemplating your imminent fate?"

"Actually, I was wondering how it is everyone knows about werewolves but not the rest of you."

Mrs. Goldeneyes lip curled. "Because they're hot-headed idiots. The wolves that belong to packs tend to be kept in line by their alphas, but they've had more than their fair share of lone wolves who just can't help themselves scaring townsfolk and carrying off women on a lark."

"And when people"—he couldn't bring himself to say humans—"find out, you kill them?"

"Not all of them. Some are ridiculed to the point they question what they think they saw. Others are drugged to make them forget. Then there are the ones that become one of us."

His eyes widened as he said, "I thought Melly said you were born this way!"

Her laughter rang out loud and sharp. "Of course, we're born. When I say become a part of, I meant merely that they're mated into the pride, sleuth, pack, or whatever group they've become aware of."

"How does that make them keep quiet?"

A golden gaze fixed him. "Because if the human betrays his or her mate, the death is a prolonged and painful one. It acts as a deterrent in most cases, and when it doesn't, a video serves as a reminder to those who might have loose lips."

It wasn't manly to gulp, and yet he did feel a bit of a tremor. His ordered world had been turned upside down. Hard to be brave when sitting alongside someone so blasé about your death.

The match started with a literal roar. Bears against lions, with the bear team a mixed blend of male and female, but on the lion's side... "It's all girls."

"Did he just call the Baddest Biatches girls?" someone shout-whispered behind him.

"Only the best play for the team," Mrs. Goldeneyes announced with pride. "I was a line blocker in my prime. Melly, being more petite on account of my husband's side, is fast, hence her position as running back."

There were no helmets, no padding, not even any cleats, only bare feet, tiny gym shorts and tank tops. The lions wore gold and black, the bears red and white.

What followed was the most violent game of rugby ever, because this wasn't the football he grew up with. There were no referees or flag on plays. Just a boisterous gamesmanship that had him on the edge of his seat.

The sheer raw strength and power was astonishing, but even more enthralling and heart stopping was watching Melly play. She seemed smaller than many out there, but she was fast, plucking the ball midair and sprinting like the wind. When she scored, he wasn't the only one stomping his feet and whistling.

By the end of the first quarter, they were ahead by two touchdowns and on fire. Toward the end of the second quarter, with the lions only up by a touchdown, their quarterback was taken out. The blow from the sizeable player lifted Robin straight off her feet. She might have recovered if she'd let go of the ball, but she didn't, and so the bears piled on. A groaning Robin had to be carried off the field.

He gaped. but Mrs. Goldeneyes snorted. "She's fine but a pussy. In my day, it took broken bones before we gave up."

A time-out was called and much hand waving by the huddled team.

"Do they have another QB?" he asked.

"Nope." Mrs. Goldeneyes popped the P with too much pleasure.

As the third quarter started, two people tried to play the position and not only got sacked, they were picked off. Suddenly the bears were up by a touchdown and a field goal. The dire situation wasn't helped by Mrs. Goldeneyes asking someone to fetch her a plastic tarp for the blood.

"I need to talk to Melly," he muttered, rising from his spot beside mama lion.

"Best say your goodbyes now. I'll want to finish you quick so I don't miss the start of dinner," she said with a cheery wave and a smile.

He shoved his hands into his pockets as he headed down to the lion bench where Melly was pacing and freaking.

"Surely one of you biatches can throw a ball downfield."

Judging by the shaking heads, none of them were willing. Melly spotted him, and her face illuminated for a moment, the happiness at the sight of him not feigned. Real. Warm. And about to be cut short.

She pulled him aside. "Listen, if things don't turn around, meet me by the edge of the woods and we'll make a run for it."

"Do you really think your mother will let me escape?" He arched a brow.

She blew out a noisy sigh. "No. But I can't just let her claw your throat open either."

"Surely someone will stop her."

Melly glanced over her shoulder where her mother held court. "Don't count on it. The only person that might be able to is Arik."

"Your lion king? Can't we ask him for sanctuary or something?"

"We could," she said slowly.

"But?"

"He kind of wants you dead, too."

"I thought he was married to a human."

"He is, and they're very much in love."

Implying he and Melly weren't. "Who says we're not?"

"Do you love me?" she asked softly.

"I don't know." He had to be honest. "But I want to find out, which means we have to win this game." He glanced at the field. "What's it take to become a part of the team?"

"You have someone in mind?"

He'd regret this probably. Might even die. "You're looking at an ex-college football star."

She blinked. "You?"

"Yes, me. I still have the record at my school for most completed passes, I'll have you know."

"You know how to play against your kind. We're talking about lions and bears here."

"I am very much aware."

"They could pulverize you on that field."

"Yes. But if I'm going to die, I'd rather it be fighting."

Melly's lower lip was sucked in as she pondered his offer. The rest of the team had no qualms.

"Let the boy play! We'll keep him safe," Joan announced.

"Well?" he asked.

"Let's go kick some bear ass."

CHAPTER SEVENTEEN

It was crazy and awesome all at once. She and Theo might have been thrust together and accidentally mated, yet there was something right about him stepping up, wanting to fight for their future together.

Of course, her mother didn't see it that way. She was the first one to call out a wager against him. "All-paid vacation to Tahiti to the first person who takes out the human quarterback."

To Melly's surprise, Auntie was the one to offer a counter. "I'm going to wager my Colorado chalet against your Bahamas condo that not only will the lions win this game but that we do it by at least two touchdowns."

With the stakes so high, a flurry of betting began, which Theo appeared to ignore. Once he'd offered to join the team, he'd only had a half-second to voice a protest as hands tore his shirt from him—which almost resulted in some biatches getting their faces torn off. Then his pants were ripped away—which did get the ass-pinching Natalya tossed into the sidelines—leaving him clad in boxers. One of the players with thicker thighs loaned him her spare pair of shorts. The tank top fit him nicely, and more than one of the biatches eyed his upper body with admiration. Enough Melly had to snarl at them to back off.

Mine.

All mine.

But in order to keep him, they had to win this game.

It took a few plays before he lost some of his stiffness. It had to be daunting knowing he was the only fragile human amidst bloodthirsty shifters, yet he kept his cool, pulling a first down on their third play, surprising everyone by darting into an opening and running eleven yards. Smart man knew to throw himself to the ground before he could get tackled.

A few downs later, he threw a pass, a beautiful long one that got batted down. But knowing what he was capable of, Melly ensured she put herself into the right spot and caught the next one. She got tackled right away, but it didn't matter. They'd gained thirty yards. After that, all she had to do was catch his eye a moment before the snap. Depending on the tilt of his head, she chose a direction to sprint.

Run. Run. Leap. Grab. Her lioness told her what to do, and she listened, hands reaching up blindly and gripping the ball when it would have passed through them.

She hit the ground with a grin and ran for a touch-down. By the middle of the last quarter, they were only down by three points. They stuffed the bears quick when it was their turn then marched themselves to a field goal.

The game was tied.

She really hoped mother was sweating. She couldn't help sending a smirk at her, to which her mother replied with an arched brow and a mouthed, "It's not over yet."

It was as if their exchange tweaked fate's tail. The next play she could only watch in horror as Percy barreled through the biatches, aiming for Theo, who threw the ball at the bear's head. It bounced just as those ham-sized fists swung.

Theo ducked but lost his glasses in the process.

Crunch. Percy ground his foot onto them as he offered a non-apologetic, "Oops."

If anything, it only firmed Theo's resolve. On their next huddle, he eyed them all, serious as he said, "Melly and Joan, run long. Natalya and Bethany, I want you both to weave."

"What about me?" asked Meena.

"How do you feel about making a grown man cry?"

As it turned out, Meena felt quite good about it, which led to a sobbing Percy being led from the field, holding his brutalized nut sac. More than one male in the crowd winced in sympathy. But it served as a warning—touch Theo and pay the price.

Melly cast a peek over at her mother and aunt. Perhaps it was a trick of the light, but she could have sworn her mother's lips held the hint of a smile. Surely not. She'd made it clear she wanted Theo gone. Melly couldn't worry about her mother's thoughts. The game still needed to be won.

As with all games of import, it came down to the last play. Ten seconds left on the clock. They were still tied and had marched that ball to within fifteen yards of the goal line. They could have kicked for a field goal, but Theo shook his head.

"We need to make this a decisive win."

"We just need to win," Melly grumbled.

He eyed her. "We do this *my* way."

The biatches oohed at his commanding tone, which caused him to blush.

Melly nodded. "Fine."

Everyone took their spot. The ball snapped, and Theo backed up, looking for a clear pass. Only Melly was covered, as was everyone else in the end zone.

So what did her stupid geek do? Ran into the end zone, scored a touchdown, then converted it into two points.

The lions went wild until Percy, having recovered, bellowed, "Don't get so excited. There's still three seconds left on the clock."

Seriously?

They could have grounded the ball to run out the clock, but honor said they had to give the bears their last miserable chance. She saw her aunt whisper something to Theo, who then had a chat with their kicker. She should have expected what came next. An onside kick. And her dumbass mate was the one to get his hands on it.

He ran down the field, the bears taking a moment to regroup and converge. As they neared, Theo jumped and soared and, as he was midair, caught her eye and winked.

He bloody well winked before tossing her the ball. Instinct had her catching it and running it in for a touchdown. With Melly busy getting her back slapped, it took a moment to realize she couldn't see Theo. Not under the pile of bodies that had pounced him.

"Get off him!" she hollered, not caring about the game anymore.

She and the biatches began pitching bodies left and right until she found a very still body at the bottom.

"Theo." She murmured his name as she sank to her knees beside him, afraid to touch him. What if she caused more damage? He wasn't made of the same stern stuff lions were.

"Is he dead?" her mother asked, having left her seat to join them staring at Melly's unconscious mate.

Melly shot her a dark look. "You'd like that, wouldn't you?"

"Not really. The boy's got good genes for a human. Did you know he scored almost perfectly on his SATs and was top of his class in the military? They discharged him over bad eyesight. Idiots. They should have given him laser surgery."

Melly stared at her mother. "You researched him?"

"Please. I have all the men you sleep with researched. Can't have you consorting with the wrong type."

"Like a human."

"Actually, I meant wrong as in morally. I can't abide a liar and a cheat. I don't think you'll have that problem with him. He's so straight he makes even rulers look crooked."

"Are you actually giving me your blessing?"

"I better if you're ever going to give me any grand-children."

"Once you have babies, you are more than welcome to vacation at my new condo in the Bahamas," Auntie declared. "Such a good boy."

Melly glared. "This is your fault, isn't it?"

"Can I help it if your man likes to win?"

"What did you promise him?"

"Passes to the front of the line at the new Disney *Star Wars* land."

"He could have died."

"But didn't and, in the process, proved himself tough enough to belong to this family."

A groan from the ground drew her attention as Theo stirred.

Melly still feared touching him. "Theo, talk to me. Tell me where you're hurt."

He rolled to his back with his eyes closed. "Everywhere."

"I'll carry you to the house so we can check you over and bandage you."

He pried one eye open. "Don't you dare. I will walk on my own two feet, thank you."

"Nice to see there's a bit of cocky male in there," her mother retorted before standing. "If you'll excuse me, I see a bear holding my place in line for those ribs."

And by holding she meant she grabbed the bulky male, tossed him to the side, and took his place. No one argued. Mother's reputation wasn't often tested, but apparently, she could still surprise.

Melly murmured, "I can't believe she's okay with us being together."

"She didn't have a choice given we won the bet," he declared, moving to a seated position.

"We only won because she allowed it."

"Allowed it how? She couldn't know I was going to step in to help."

"Don't be so sure of that." With mother doing a background check, she would have known about his past football career and tested to see what kind of man he was.

The kind a lioness could love.

"What do you say we skip dinner and go straight to dessert?" she asked.

Silly man thought she meant sex. When she actually meant dessert. Only when she'd filled two large plates with one of everything did they escape to the attic. She ate one plate on the way, meaning she was ready to strip once the hatch to her room shut.

In her cramped shower, he allowed her to inspect every inch of his fine body. Kiss every bruise. Lick every scratch. Then suck on the part of him that needed easing.

Then it was her turn. He licked every sensitive inch. Sucked on her nipples and the spot between her legs. Thrust his fingers into her as he swirled his tongue around her puckered nubs. Then finally slid into her, inches of glorious hardness filling her to perfection, and when she came so hard her toes curled and she uttered a tiny roar, he said, "I love you."

"Me, too, but FYI, touch the pecan pie on the nightstand and I will tear out your guts."

Then she proceeded to show him how much she enjoyed said pie by licking it off his dick.

When they emerged a few hours later, looking for food, there was a cheer from the drunken lions and bears under the patio lanterns strung all around.

"Theo, you straight-laced bastard! Come drink with us!"

She lost him for a while as he was feted and given beer and other alcoholic beverages. When it was time for bed, she hunted down her lightweight mate, who sat leaning on a tree, almost passed out

He smiled and slurred, "I finally see why people love cats. Come close so I can pet your pussy."

He sobered right quick when he felt the fur under his fingers, and when he fell asleep wrapped around her, it was better than a warm patch of sun.

Melly crouched on the roof, wearing her dark spandex uniform, a bodysuit the biatches had designed for stealthy missions at night. No longer did they entertain themselves with bar fights and chicken races on the highway. They had actual jobs now, working for the Internal Revenue Service.

Not that the IRS was aware that they'd officially hired the Baddest Biatches. With Theo having cracked Marney's weapons ring, he got a promotion, which was when Arik got the bright idea of having Theo as their inside liaison to keep them safe.

What better way to keep Theo moving up in the ranks than to ensure he kept cracking the hardest cases? With a little pride help, he found the biggest cheaters on taxes. Busting them only increased his reputation, and given the biatches only went after crooks, no one noticed the bits skimmed off the top to fund some of their pricier purchases.

Which her number-loving husband liked to question. *"Why do we need another flamethrower?"*

"What if the first one breaks?"

"Let me guess, the helicopter you put the deposit on is for parachuting missions."

"Nah, that's for pure fun."

Funny how he didn't argue when she bought him an authentic Vader costume from the original movie set.

Life was good for this lioness, especially since she could be herself with her partner, best friend, and lover.

Rawr.

AUTHOR'S NOTE: So, I know this book took a while to come out, mostly because I like to wait until stories talk to me. But the funny thing was, when I began writing it, I got an idea for two more Lion's Pride stories.

How do these sound?

SOMEWHERE IN THE WORLD...

The glass door shattered, but Dean didn't pause as he took a sip of the amber whiskey he'd just poured.

A figure swung into the room, arriving by a rope that they snapped loose as they landed on their feet. The slight figure didn't hold any weapon, and a dark hood hid their features.

But he didn't need to see to know.

"Hello, Natasha. Long time, no see."

"Don't you mean since our wedding night?" She swung her hips as she stalked toward him.

Less wedding, more drunken hoax. "What's it been, five years, six?" He could have quoted the exact time down to the minute had he wished. As if he'd give her that kind of power.

"Too long and overdue. I'm here to ask for a divorce."

He arched a brow. "Is this where I say I believe the vow was until death do you part?"

"If you insist."

COMING WHEN YOU LEAST EXPECT IT, WHEN A TIGON WEDS.

AND FOR THE NEXT TEASER...

The pinprick in his arm was like the smallest of stings. There and gone, not even worth his attention.

But perhaps Lawrence should have minded it because his senses clouded, his vision filmed over, and when next he regained consciousness, it was to find himself in a strange cabin in bed with a woman.

A human and—judging by the scent on her and the marks at her neck—his mate.

LAWRENCE'S STORY IS COMING SOON IN WHEN A LIGER MATES.

Previous books in A Lion's Pride, a USA Today Bestselling series:

Be sure to visit www.EveLanglais for more books with furry heroes, or sign up for the Eve Langlais newsletter for notification about new stories or specials.